I hope you enjoy this new series, Dora.

HARMONY HOUSE

RUTH HAY

Ruth Hay.

June 2018.

HARMONY HOUSE
BY RUTH HAY

It was a wonderful plan. A plan to solve all their problems and provide an old age designed exactly to their requirements. But the plan had a flaw. It would not work for just two women. Partners would be required. Several partners.

The person who has lived the most is not the one with the most years but the one with the richest experiences. Jean-Jacques Rousseau

CHAPTER 1

Hilary and Mavis decided at long last, that the only way to accomplish their objective was to write an advert and post copies in the local shop, the library and the grocery store.

"For pity's sake, Hilary, how are we going to compose an advertisement without sounding like a pair of crazy old women?"

"I think a little madness at this juncture might not be a bad thing, Mavis. After all, we don't wish to attract just anyone. We need like-minded females with some spark about them. We can be quite specific about our requirements and that will scare away the weird ones."

Mavis looked sceptical. She was imagining a troupe of women appearing at their door and being turned away as completely unsuitable. She was not going to be the one who did the job of dismissing the unsuccessful candidates. Let Hilary do that part. She had been a school principal and knew how to deliver bad news when necessary. Hilary had been the one to break the awful news about Mavis'ss husband's death years before and she had held tight to her friend until the heaving sobs diminished. There had been a special bond between the two since then. As usual, Mavis must just trust her.

She took a deep breath and continued.

"Well then, let me hear what you have in mind."

Hilary picked up the pen from her desk and began to write on a thick pad of lined paper.

Several minutes went by before she looked up again.

"Right! What do you think about this?"

She read aloud the following list.

- Female companions required to share spacious accommodations.
- Must have sound finances, good health, sociable personalities and willingness to try something different.
- Candidates should prepare to be vetted before being accepted.

If you are interested, meet the undersigned at 46, Camden Corners, London, Ontario, at 1:00pm Saturday, November 15, 2016.

Hilary Dempster. Mavis Montgomery. Please call us to assure us of your attendance.

Mavis had to admit her friend had hit the nail on the head at first try.

"I think it's rather good. Not too long or too detailed. Just the pertinent facts. But I think it needs a catchy title to draw attention on a crowded bulletin board."

"Good idea! What do you suggest?"

This part demanded more thinking and no little amount of creativity. Eventually they agreed on the finished format and Hilary undertook to type the ad on her computer and print the copies on cardstock for immediate use. Mavis added a delicate floral drawing around the edges to make the card stand out.

"No point in delaying. Mavis. We have made the decision and now we need to see if our plan will work for us."

∽

In due time the advert was placed on the selected bulletin boards and the couple waited to hear if there were any replies.

A week went by and Mavis began to worry.

"Do you think the title might have been disturbing?"

"What's disturbing about 'Once-in-a-Lifetime Opportunity'?"

"It might be construed as an insurance scheme or a timeshare or a hoax of some kind."

Hilary put her cup down carefully on the china saucer and considered her friend's comment.

"I suppose someone might be put off by the title but then, we don't want anyone who can't see a good opportunity like this. If a person were to be reluctant to read further, we wouldn't likely find them suitable in any case."

"Perhaps not. It's just a shame that we haven't had any replies at all."

"It's possible we haven't tried the right places yet. We could advertise further afield but local women would be more amenable to living in this city, I suspect. They would be familiar with their surroundings rather than having to get used to a new town. We will have to be patient."

Another week went by and Hilary was considering retrieving the ads and changing the date of the proposed meeting. On the very next day, four women called to reserve a place. Hilary was shopping in town when the calls came.

"Hello, this is Victoria Simons. I am calling about the advert for women to share housing. I would like to attend the meeting."

Mavis quickly found the pen and paper Hilary had left ready by the phone with a note reminding them which questions to ask.

"Yes. May I have your name again?"

"Victoria Simons. Call me Vicky. Actually, I am calling on behalf of myself and my friend Lorna Wallace."

"I see. Have you read all the requirements listed in the advert?"

"We have, and we are very intrigued by the whole idea. Can you give us more information?"

"No. You will be able to ask all your questions at the meeting. Do you know the house?"

"I have a GPS on my car so I am sure I will find you. See you on the 15th?"

"Yes. We look forward to meeting you then."

Hilary's notes included instructions to supply any hints about the caller so as to prepare Hilary ahead of time. Mavis wrote down beside the names;

2 friends One drives and has a GPS Possibly not living in this area No detectable clues.

She had scarcely finished writing when the phone rang again.

"Is this the house where the meeting is to take place? I wrote the number down but it got smudged in the bottom of my purse....some water leaked I think. I am not sure if I have it right. Is this the house?"

"Are you replying to the advert on a bulletin board?"

"Oh, yes. I was wandering around in the library yesterday. It was raining and I was waiting for a bus so I popped in for a couple of minutes and then I was reading the announcements and stuff and there it was. I was amazed, I can tell you. Talk about something coming along at just the right time? Honestly, not buses of course. They are usually late aren't they?"

The woman paused to take a breath and Mavis jumped in quickly before she galloped off on another tangent. "May I have your name?"

"Right. Of course. It's Jannice O'Connor, two n's in the middle. In Jannice as well, as it happens! Does this mean I can come to the meeting? Oh, I would be so, so grateful. I love your idea. Living alone is so…. Well it's hard to describe. Am I in?"

"Well, Jannice, I can reserve a place for you. Do you have a note of the address and all the other information on the card?"

"Yes, I have it all somewhere. I need to work out the bus times but I am definitely coming. On the 15th, right?"

"Right! We'll see you then, Jannice."

"Thank you. Thank you so very much."

Talkative Lonely? A bit distracted Keen on the idea Arriving by bus

Mavis was about to add something about a possible Irish accent when she heard the front door open and Hilary's voice complaining about the rain for the third day in a row.

"Any calls?"

"Actually, yes. There were two calls and three candidates."

"Excellent news!"

Hilary arrived in the family room shedding her scarf and anxiously examining the paper pad by the phone.

"Well, isn't this reassuring, Mavis? There is some interest in our idea after all."

Before she could say more, the phone by her hand rang again. Quirking her eyebrow in Mavis's direction, she picked up the receiver and said, 'Hi, who's calling?"

"Oh, it's me. I mean I think I recognize your voice. It's Hilary. Am I right?"

"Yes, Hilary is correct but I'm afraid I don't recognize *your* voice."

"It's been a long time. This is Jo. I thought the accent might strike a chord."

"Jo? I'm sorry. I don't recall the name. Wait a minute. Do you mean Josette?"

"Yes, Josette Delacour, as I used to be, and am again now."

There was one of those silences they call 'pregnant' in novels. Hilary's mind was racing. In the far distant past she had known a Josette Delacour and the relationship had not ended well.

"I see. What can I do for you, Josette?"

"I saw your advert and I wondered if you would have space for an old friend in your house."

Hilary cast her eyes upward to where Mavis was standing listening avidly.

"*What should I do?*" she whispered. Mavis signalled approval with a firm nod of her head.

"Well then, please come along and hear our story and you can decide for yourself. I don't expect we can accommodate everyone who asks but we'll see how it goes."

"That's all I ask, Hil. I'll be there. *Au revoir!*"

"Well, I guess we won't need notes to recognize that lady? Did you know her well? She called you Hil, pronounced 'Heel' in her accent. You never let anyone call you Hil and certainly not 'heel'."

"My dear, you have very good hearing. I will tell you later when………………"

Both women jumped as the phone rang again.

"It never rains but it pours, it seems," commented Mavis. "Shall I take this one? I hope there won't be too many more."

It was to be the final call of the day. Mavis listened, and wrote some notes and when she put the phone down again she had a puzzled look on her face.

"What now?"

"I don't know exactly. The woman was speaking very quietly and urgently. She didn't say much at all. She gave her name as Eve Barton but she stumbled over the last name as if she was not familiar with it.

She lives in town but really wants to attend the meeting. She said she might be a little late arriving."

The two friends looked at each other. Both were thinking they had put something in motion and now the idea was becoming a reality. Other lives were involved. Other people's futures were in their hands. Choices had to be made; decisions that could impact their own lives. It became imperative to organize the meeting on November 15 so that the best decisions were made on the basis of very little information. This meeting was going to affect every person involved for the rest of their lives.

CHAPTER 2

I t did not surprise Mavis to find that Hilary had prepared a card for each candidate. She had left space for comments and at the bottom of the card, choices were to be checked: Accept / Possible / No

The week prior to the 15th was occupied with a variety of options relating to achieving as much information as possible from the women.

"We have given them the important headings already, Mavis. They won't be coming if they don't qualify in the financial and health areas. "

"There could be problems when they discover how much money is required."

"You are right about that."

Mavis looked out of the kitchen window. She still had doubts about leaving her own home in which she had lived for decades. She knew Hilary was thinking of their future and her decisions were indisputably beneficial to both of them, but sometimes she wondered if another choice would be preferable.

She adjusted the flowers in the vase on the centre of the table. By the time flowers grew once more in this garden, Mavis would no longer be an occupant, if all the plans went ahead. In the meantime she spent more time at Hilary's larger home while all the arrangements were being made. It was easier that way.

"Anything else on your mind, dear? You seem thoughtful."

"Yes. I was wondering how we could judge the sociability factor." She turned to face her companion. Now was not the time to express doubts to Hilary. That time had passed.

"I did have an idea about that. What do you think?"

The idea involved a series of games in which cooperation was involved; a simple charades game with guesses around popular television and movies, a short line dance with music and instruction supplied by Mavis, and a 'What if' quiz or a jigsaw puzzle to be attempted. Preparing for these, absorbed another day or two and suddenly, it was the day before the meeting and both women were cleaning the house, assembling cups and saucers for tea and baking some treats to share with the candidates along with reorganizing the dining room with chairs in a double row.

"We should take the extra leaf out of the table," suggested Mavis, "and move it to the wall as a kind of desk for you, Hilary. Later it can be used for the jigsaw."

"Good thinking! If you want me to take the lead I feel you would be best employed welcoming the visitors and making observations from the back of the dining room. You know you are so intuitive about atmosphere and people's reactions. Your years spent in court work gave you excellent skills in that area."

"I'll be happy to do that. So we are set up for five applicants now?"

Mavis had no sooner spoken than the phone in the kitchen shrilled and, simultaneously, Hilary's phone in her pocket jangled its insistent call. When the two women reassembled, they had surprising news.

Two new candidates, making seven in all.

"Who called you?" they said together, and laughed aloud.

"Mine is a woman who decided at the last minute. Her name is Honor Pace."

"My call was from a Vilma Smith who just saw the ad today and didn't want to miss a chance to be included."

"What do we do now? With the two of us that makes *nine women*. We can't possibly provide for that many."

"I know, Mavis, but remember we will lose some right away when they hear the plan and others may drop out before they have to make a definite commitment."

"I hope you are right. Let's find more chairs and you need to make extra cards."

～

The morning of the 15th dawned bright after an overnight frost that brought down leaves from the mature trees on the avenue. Mavis made a mental note about finding a property without too many trees. Raking and bagging leaves was an annual ritual in the Forest City but not one welcomed by those lacking considerable muscle strength, not to mention perseverance over weeks to keep at the job.

Hilary arrived early and they had a warming cup of coffee in the kitchen while they ran over the day's plans.

"We won't give anyone a definite yes or no today,

Mavis, so do not worry about that. We will gather all the information we can and take our time about what to do. As long as we are firm on the number six, we can benefit from having a wider selection from which to choose. Let's relax and try to have some fun with this."

Mavis did not think telling people they had failed to meet the test was 'fun'. She was glad that task had been claimed by Hilary. She was content to stay in the background and observe, in the knowledge that it was the place from which she could contribute the most valuable information.

The doorbell chimed at a quarter to one. Mavis was ready. She planned to make good use of the time to get to know any early arrivals. On the doorstep she found two women.

Jannice O'Connor was a small, dark-haired person wearing a coat two sizes too large and a worried expression.

"I know I am too early but I had to take an earlier bus to be sure of getting here on time. I don't know this part of London very well so I wanted to walk around for a bit. It's getting cloudy and I thought it might rain and here I am. I hope you don't mind?"

Yes, she is a talkative one. But sort of appealing, like a small child. Possibly a neglected small child?

Mavis welcomed Jannice in and took her coat then turned to the other arrival. This one turned out to be a complete contrast. Vilma Smith was elegant in style with fashionable clothes and unsuitable-for-the-weather high heels. She swept in and removed her fur-lined raincoat, hanging it in the hall closet and looking around as if to assess the owners by judging their furnishings.

Confident. Good finances. Professional skills? May challenge Hilary for control.

Mavis invited the women to help themselves to tea, coffee and muffins while they waited for the others.

Hilary joined them, so Mavis could continue to monitor the door.

Vicky Simons and Lorna Wallace arrived together and were arguing about the correct address when Mavis first saw them.

"Honestly, Lorna, you should have brought my note about the ad. I must have mentioned it five times this morning. You are really becoming very forgetful."

"If you were finding the information so necessary, Vicky, you should have done it yourself instead of blaming me."

They stumped inside, with barely concealed animosity, and decided to take seats in the dining room at opposite ends of the last row.

Troublesome pair. Why would they want to live together? Look like sisters or cousins. Same angry faces and dark colouring.

Ten more minutes went by before Eve Barton appeared from a taxi. Mavis was counting and remembered Josette Delacour had said she would be late so that left only Honor Pace unaccounted for.

Hilary was already shepherding the candidates into their seats and glancing at her watch. She expected punctuality.

Mavis stepped outside to welcome Eve Barton and when she saw her face, she was very glad she had done so. The woman wore a slouch hat pulled down on the right side of her pale face to hide a bruise layered in makeup that did not do a good job of concealment. As Mavis reached her, one glance at the quavering lips and shaking hands reminded her strongly of abused women she had often consoled in the court system.

This one needs support and sympathy, which I can certainly supply. Hope Hilary agrees with me.

She took Eve into the kitchen and poured her a cup of tea, adding sugar without asking and indicating she should stay there for a few minutes and listen to the presentation in comfort. Mavis promised to fetch her later and take her to a seat in the rear.

Hilary was waiting for a pre-arranged signal from Mavis to indicate all had arrived. Mavis showed her they were one short and Hilary nodded and began.

"Welcome ladies. Mavis and I are pleased that you answered our advertisement and were interested in finding out more about our plan. Today's meeting is about introducing each other, and seeing if we are compatible.

Mavis and I are long-time friends who have watched our menfolk sicken and die, and our families move away, leaving us to soldier on alone. We have managed this very well, all things considered, but we have also noticed this is a growing trend in society. A recent article stated as many as 1.4 million elderly Canadians who are living alone, reported feeling lonely.

Now, we two have taken the time to investigate the selection of care facilities and residential homes available in and around our fair city, and there are many of these. We have sampled their meals and toured open days. We have talked to their personnel and inspected their accommodations. We have seen their newsletters and marvelled at the range of weekly activities. We have seen common areas, swimming pools and doctors' facilities. All of these are well maintained and for those who prefer this life, for whatever reasons of health or convenience, we applaud them.

It's just not for us.

Government-assisted care homes for nursing and long term assistance are what we consider a last ditch option. For now, we feel we have the energy and finances to look at other options.

Mavis and I believe we can live independently, in comfort, with a few well-chosen friends, in one family home in London, for years to come.

Before you ask, this is not the home I mean. I live here, currently. We plan to purchase a larger home with space for six bedrooms and all the facilities required to see us through the coming years. So we need four companions on this journey. I can see questions arising already, so I will stop and answer your enquiries now."

Hilary took a sip of water from a glass, glanced at her notes, her cards, and then at Mavis who was shepherding a younger woman wearing a hat to a seat. She also noticed Josette Delacour arriving and taking her seat and thought she would definitely have recognized her anywhere. That head of vibrant fair hair always marked Jo out in a crowd even in their high school days when they had competed for the attentions of one Johnathan James Langton.

"I am wondering what financial contributions are required for the purchase of a suitable house?"

The onslaught of questions was beginning.

The elegant woman in the front row with the immaculate hairstyle, seemed to have spoken up for others as heads nodded at her enquiry.

"Mavis and I will sell our current homes and from the proceeds we each hope to contribute something above 100,000 dollars to the general pot. This sum from each participant will allow us the finances to buy a good property and also to customize it to some degree for considerations of aging, such as an elevator and assistance from outside help as needed."

This was the crucial point that would separate the simply curious from the definitely interested.

So far it was taking a few moments for the financial information to sink in.

Unexpectedly, a small, bird-like woman in dingy clothing spoke up. She had a quiet voice with a lilting Irish accent, but everyone in the dining room heard her appeal.

"How soon do you wish to have the money in place?"

Mavis thought, *Jannice is anxious to be included. Will she have sufficient funds for this?*

Hilary glanced at her cards. "Jannice, that is an excellent question. Of course, if your current properties are to be sold it will require time. There may be some of you who have the finances available already and if so, the money may be placed with an estate lawyer for safe-keeping until the required amount is obtained.

Jannice smiled a tiny smile and in the back row, the lady wearing the hat looked relieved.

A young woman at one end of the same row stood abruptly and stated she was unable to meet the cash demands and she and her cousin would now be leaving. The cousin, who looked enough alike to be a sister, looked shocked, but followed her out to the front hall where Mavis quickly retrieved their coats and wished them well. They exited as they had arrived, arguing together about such a ridiculous, time-wasting idea.

Hilary was now facing just four remaining candidates. She knew Josette and Jannice for sure, but was not certain about the names of the two others. One must be Vilma Smith or Honor Pace and the other Eve Barton.

This is working out much better than I had expected but it's too soon to be counting our chickens.

Mavis returned and sized up the situation. She went to the front and introduced Hilary to Eve

Barton and Vilma Smith, then she discreetly removed the cards for Vicky Simons and Lorna Wallace and wrote a question mark against the name of Honor Pace, who had not yet arrived.

"I suggest we move the table forward and sit around it to answer further questions and perhaps play a game or two, if you are willing."

The new arrangement was soon put in place, and Mavis brought out a tray with drinks and pastries to speed conversation. She exchanged a meaningful glance with Hilary as she took her seat.

Now we are on our way at last.

CHAPTER 3

Although the numbers were right, there was still a long way to go before final decisions could be made. It started over hot drinks and treats but soon became more about life stories and future concerns.

The questions continued.

In which part of London were they thinking of finding a house?

Building or buying?

Country or city?

Old or new property?

What kind of bedrooms were they looking for?

Shared bathrooms or ensuite?

Kitchen facilities?

House rules?

Hilary's general response was to say these decisions would be made together and would depend on the amount of money at their disposal.

Eve Barton seemed to favour a house outside the city while Jannice O'Connor was alarmed at being without access to city buses. Hilary made a note.

Vilma Smith introduced the topic of limiting the shared facilities. She stated she had no intention of eating all her meals on someone's else's timetable and would require at least a kettle and microwave.

Mavis spoke up while Hilary made another note.

"I believe it would be useful to eat the evening meal together. Perhaps not every night but two or three times a week to keep in touch with each other."

"I really dislike cooking for others," added Josette Delacour, with a laugh. "I know, French Canadian women are supposed to live in the kitchen but my mother ruled the roost and never allowed me to learn her secrets. I rarely cook for myself preferring to eat out with a gentleman companion if possible."

She shook her fair hair into place with a sly smile as if she enjoyed the impact her statements made on the others.

Hilary suspected Jo was not joking about the male companion. In school she had the reputation of chasing other girls' boyfriends and never buying herself as much as a coke or ice cream. Jo was responsible for breaking up a promising romance of Hilary's with these tactics. It appeared she had not changed much since those long-ago days.

Mavis cleared her throat and stated the objective was for each person to live her own life but with the benefit of shared tasks and the opportunity to talk to and enjoy company whenever it might be desired.

"After all," she concluded, "if a woman wanted to live a totally separate life, an apartment in a large building would be sufficient."

"I agree," stated Jannice, speaking quickly and quietly. "I have lived my life as a carer for my mother and father. I rarely saw anyone of my own age to talk to, or shop with, or go for a meal with. I do not want to be isolated for the rest of my days. I have had enough of that. Now I need my own good life with pleasant companions around me."

It was becoming obvious to Hilary that Jannice's style of rapid talking was because of the situation she had been in with ailing parents. The poor woman was starved of companionship.

Jannice's confession seemed to prompt the others to tell a bit about their lives.

The stylish woman, now identified as Vilma Smith, was the next to speak up but her story could not be more different.

"Personally speaking, I am looking for an all-female establishment. A few months ago I buried my second husband after a happy twenty years together during which time I looked after his three kids from a first marriage. Unfortunately, my step-children never left the influence of their mother and consequently they disliked me intensely. I could tolerate that dislike well enough for their father's sake but after their father died and they discovered he had left a large amount of money to me, they unleashed their full disapproval and made my life a misery. I want nothing more to do with men or their children."

This was more than the others around the table wanted to know on such short acquaintance. They looked down at their cups or fiddled with serviettes and waited, in some discomfort, to see who would dare to speak next.

Hilary filled the gap with a related question. "Vilma brings up the issue of husbands and children. How will we deal with visits from one or both categories of relatives?"

"It's not likely we could accommodate visiting relatives for any amount of time. I don't believe such family members should be inflicted on others in the same house. We can establish house rules whereby visitors should be entertained in town. No overnight visitors could be the rule."

"That sounds sensible, Josette." Mavis was pleased talk of house rules had emerged so soon. This was sure to be one of the most contentious issues but she and Hilary had decided rules were essential to the smooth operation of a joint owner-ship plan.

"Well, thank you for your honesty, ladies. I suggest we break into two or three smaller groups and get to know each other over an activity. I have a large jigsaw puzzle here and Mavis has a question-naire for each of you. Don't worry. It isn't necessary to complete it now. Just bring it to our next meeting."

There was an air of relief in the room. Mavis led the way into the comfortable living room where the seats were arranged in twos or threes around a coffee table or side table. She had placed copies of the questionnaire on each surface along with a variety of board games ready to be played. These ranged from a magnetic tic-tac-toe board to chess and bridge. She waited to see who would choose which.

Then she returned to the dining room and set out the jigsaw puzzle, leaving Hilary to observe the activity in the living room.

By the time she had found and placed the four

corner pieces, Eve Barton had taken a seat beside her.

Mavis welcomed her and asked if she was a jigsaw fan.

"Yes, I suppose I am. I began long ago to pass the time at home when my father-in-law was first ill. He was disturbed by noise and chatter. It was a quiet activity and I guess it just became a habit. It gives you time to think."

Eve Barton, adjusted her hat to further conceal the bruise on her face and apologized to Mavis.

"I am not really here for the puzzle. I feel we have a connection. You were kind to me earlier, and I need to explain something before I leave. I have a taxi waiting on a nearby street."

"Of course, Eve, you can tell me anything. I am not easily shocked."

Eve took a deep breath and swallowed convulsively before she began.

"You see, I may be here under false pretences. I am not exactly free to make the choice you require.

I am currently married to a man I have grown to hate. My escape from him became a possibility when a distant relative died leaving me a substantial sum of money. My husband knows nothing of this and I hope to leave him and begin a new life. I am not fit to live alone, however. I feel I need support and friendship until I can recover from what has happened in the past. I am telling you this, Mavis, because I must go now and I am hoping you will give me a chance to be included in your project."

Mavis made no comment. She hid her dismay and stood at once, handing Eve a questionnaire and telling her the date of their next meeting as she helped her on with her coat.

"Please come next time, Eve. I can promise you a safe haven here. Take care."

Eve Barton turned with tears in her eyes. It was so long since she had heard such words of comfort that she reached for Mavis and gave her a brief hug before rushing down the steps and off into the street.

Mavis stood watching her until she had disappeared.

Her emotions were in turmoil. She felt such empathy for the woman and hoped she had done the right thing by encouraging her. Hilary might have a very different view of accepting into their future home, a woman with such baggage. Mavis had acted on impulse and she felt very strongly about sticking by her word even if there was an argument pending.

She stepped quietly into the living room and was reassured by the sound of laughter. Hilary and Vilma were competing over the tic-tac-toe board.

They seemed to be doing a speed contest and Vilma was winning. Mavis was pleased these two dominant personalities were taking each other's measure. If they were to be sharing a house, it was essential that mutual respect be established as soon as possible.

Hilary looked up as Mavis entered and they exchanged an enquiring glance. Hilary nodded happily, but Mavis contributed a frown alerting her friend to trouble.

At a side table, Josette and Jannice had abandoned their card game and were now in deep conversation. Jannice's face showed amazement at whatever tale her companion was spinning.

Mavis hoped it was not some incident from their schooldays that would be embarrassing to Hilary.

She took the nearest chair and listened in. *Best to be forewarned.*

"........and then he picked me up and swung me around and my foot hit the vase of flowers which clattered onto the floor spilling roses and water everywhere. We couldn't stop laughing long enough to clear it up, so we went off to bed and left the mess there until the morning. It was *très amusante!*"

Mavis decided to step in before Jannice was even more shocked.

She looked at the carriage clock on Hilary's

mantel and saw it was time to draw the session to a close.

She collected up the spare questionnaire copies and Hilary took the hint.

"Thank you all so much for coming today. We hope to see you back here in one week. Mavis has your homework assignment and we will have more opportunities to answer questions when you have had time to consider your answers."

The three women collected their coats and went off down the steps smiling, waving and exchanging information about how they had travelled to the house. Vilma and Josette had driven cars from opposite parts of London. Vilma volunteered to give Jannice a ride home and save her from the long and weary bus trip.

"Nobody's waiting at home for me to arrive, Jannice. I'll be happy to take you."

Once the driveway was empty of cars, Mavis closed the front door and went to hear what Hilary thought about their first meeting.

"Well, Mavis, we have taken on quite a daunting task. I have the measure of Mrs. Vilma Smith and she is a forceful character all right, but that's not necessarily a bad thing. I know the type of woman

Josette is, and of the two, she is likely to be more trouble in the long run. I did not have much opportunity to talk with the other two women. What's your opinion about them?"

Mavis took a seat at the kitchen island and waited until her friend had poured fresh tea into her cup. It was a time for brutal honesty.

"I am in agreement with your evaluation of Vilma and Josette but we have a serious issue with the two remaining women for entirely different reasons."

"Oh, that sounds ominous. Tell me."

"Jannice is of lesser concern. She is like a child who has been kept under such control for so many years she is barely functioning as an adult. I feel she would be very easily swayed by any of us and perhaps be unable to live comfortably as an individual with equal weight and responsibility."

Hilary blinked and focussed fully on Mavis. She had great respect for her friend's ability to see within people and discern their motives, but this assessment had been predicated as 'of lesser concern'. What was to come next?"

"As for Eve Barton, I must confess I have tremendous sympathy for her situation, Hilary, but she is trouble with a capital T."

"I am surprised to hear this. What has brought you to this conclusion?"

There was no point in sugar coating the truth. Mavis waded right in.

"She told me she is married to an abuser. You saw the evidence on her face. She is hoping to run away from her husband and take up a new life with us, using money from an inheritance."

"Oh my! *That is* a problem! I take it you are suggesting this man would not be happy with her choice?"

"As far as I can tell, he knows nothing of her intentions. If we choose Eve Barton we would probably be caught up in a possible legal mess with a violent man and a damaged and cowed woman."

CHAPTER 4

Jannice O'Connor felt completely out of place in the luxurious car of Vilma Smith. Sitting this closely, she could smell both the new car leather scent and also the expensive perfume the lady wore. Jannice tugged at her ill-fitting, old clothes and tried to cover up the stains on her coat which she feared might contaminate the atmosphere in the warmth of this beautiful vehicle.

She listened as Vilma commented on the weather, the traffic, the meeting they had both been to and her own situation. Fortunately, Vilma did not require a response from her passenger. Jannice was feeling most uncomfortable. She did not own a car, or fancy clothes. All she had in the world was the ancient furniture in the ancient run-down

O'Connor house and an accumulation of the detritus of decades of living that crowded the place with memories that were not all happy. She still felt amazed that she had had the courage to read the advert on the grocery store bulletin board, phone the number, seek out a bus service and actually turn up at the house on the right date and time. It was the first totally independent thing she had done in the last thirty years. For an entire year after her mother died, she had existed in a fog of indecision in the house she detested, and done nothing about her situation. It had taken that long for her to realize she was alone with a future ahead for which she would have to forge a plan.

Now she had taken the first bold step and she was still undecided. Would these bright, capable women want her with them on a permanent basis? Would the house she had lived in all her life provide sufficient funds for the lifestyle she wished to achieve?

As Vilma prattled on about her evil stepchildren, Jannice realized she must make a start on clearing out the O'Connor house. Just the thought made her start to sweat. For so many years nothing had been done to maintain 109, Fairset Road. There was a bedroom upstairs used as a repository for anything in the way, or broken beyond repair. Jannice had not been inside that room for a very long time. And then there was the basement piled to the ceiling in parts. Her heart quailed at the thought of all these decisions awaiting her, and yet, at the same time there was excitement at the prospect of creating a more livable space, not for herself, of course. She was finished with that old life. Improvements would be for the new family who would buy the house from her.

"Don't you find that to be true, Jannice?"

She was jolted back to the present and said the first thing that entered her mind.

"Absolutely!" It seemed to be sufficient to satisfy Vilma.

Jannice looked around and recognized that she was now close to the Old East London area where she lived.

As a non-driver, she was unable to give directions to Vilma but she noticed a device on the dash of the car on which a moving plan of the local streets was pointing the driver to her address.

She quickly exited the car and thanked Vilma for her kindness. She did not want to answer any questions or even accept a ride for the next meeting. She would take the bus again and set out early.

Taking the keys out of her pocket, she approached the front door with trepidation. After the neat and clean home of Hilary Dempster, she was sure the interior of 109, was going to be a disappointment.

She opened the door and stepped inside and was immediately assaulted in all her senses.

Lord help me! I did not realize what was happening in here. I have been living blind for so long. I have been living in a hoarder's mess without seeing it!

Vilma was not expecting an invitation to Jannice's home. She would never consider leaving her valuable automobile in such a street, even for a few minutes. Really, it was a miserable looking place of row houses with untidy gardens and windows that badly needed a good scrub. She had heard about London's Old East but not had any reason to venture there. It was a sketchy sort of place that had undergone a series of changes over the years, all designed to improve its image, but judging from what she saw in front of her, some parts had evaded those attempts.

She turned and drove off rapidly, wondering how Jannice O'Connor, a woman on her own, would recoup the sum of $100,000 from her unprepossessing property in order to claim a place in the shared home.

It was not until she had returned to the more affluent streets of Sunningdale, in North London, that she felt at ease again.

Nothing could be more different than her current residence with its double driveway leading to a spacious garage and the front entrance that wowed visitors and set them up for the grand, high-ceilinged rooms, impressive staircase and amazing décor throughout.

She took pride in the last of these elements as she had been responsible for the styling of the property when she and Nolan bought this house in the new subdivision several years before.

As she looked around now, the sparkle had gone from her surroundings. This home was in dispute. Nolan's children were banding together to contest her husband's will. She had thought long and hard about her response. She could battle them in the courts for years but she had decided to relinquish the beautiful home without complaining, in a bid to keep the considerable amount of cash Nolan had left to her. The children, now grown adults, could do what they wished as long as they left her to her own devices.

She foresaw years of arguments over who would occupy this home while she would be free to find a living plan of her own choice. Let them have it. She wanted nothing to do with any of the selfish, stubborn family who had clung to their mother and set themselves against Vilma from the start.

She kicked off her shoes and climbed the staircase to the master suite and her dressing room closets. Time to decide which of her outfits would go to the consignment store and which she would keep for her new accommodations. She might never have this kind of space around her again for her possessions but she hoped instead for comfort, and company, and far less responsibility. She already liked Hilary's spark and that quiet Mavis who clearly had more to her than appeared on the surface.

A new start was overdue for Vilma Smith and that tall set of shelves holding very expensive shoes was the place to begin.

Eve Barton saw her cab waiting for her on a side street, as arranged. She did not want the driver to see the address of Hilary's house. She had been developing a secretive style ever since she had consulted the bank manager about the inheritance and that sympathetic lady had advised her to open an account of her own, separate from that of her husband.

Not that Howard Dobrinski was all that interested in his wife's activities. As long as she had a meal ready when he arrived home from drinking with his buddies, and was there to serve as a punching bag whenever things at work were not to his pleasing, he chose to ignore her.

It had not always been like this. Before the drinking started, they had a pleasant enough marriage. No better, or worse, than that of any of their former friends. Privately, Eve put the blame on her inability to have children as the start of the downturn. Not that she hadn't tried. Three debilitating miscarriages in a row had knocked down her confidence and her physical strength. When her doctor insisted on a six month waiting period before she tried again, Howard complained bitterly and cursed the doctor for trying to deny him his rights as a husband.

Eve felt that was the beginning of her mental separation from her husband. His lack of concern for her physical wellbeing was like a piece of ice settling in her soul. When he refused to consider adoption saying, 'He was not about to take on another man's unwanted brat' the ice began to grow and the drinking and physical abuse made the gulf between them seem impassible. From time to time she attempted to bridge the gap, but it was too late.

She retreated from all social events in fear of

awkward questions. Soon she was a prisoner in her own home; a prisoner who could not contemplate a future that was so lacking in the warmth of human kindness.

She was seriously thinking of putting an end to her life when the letter enclosing a cheque arrived.

At first she thought it must be some wicked joke or a scam of some kind but when no phone calls came demanding money from her, she began to wonder if it might be a miraculous way out of her miserable existence. She made a quick trip to the bank one morning with the cheque in hand and as she stepped out onto the street after her interview with the bank manager, it was as if the sun came out and the birds began to sing and the ice in her soul finally began to melt. It was only a few weeks later, when she saw the advert in the local library, that she could begin to dream of a new life again. But every part of the dream had to be kept completely secret.

Eve asked the cab driver to let her out at the strip mall where she had called him to pick her up. She paid the fare in cash and quickly walked to a corner store where she bought some groceries in case Howard came home early and quizzed her about her absence.

To her relief, the house was empty and she was able to sit in peace in her bedroom with the questionnaire in hand and consider her answers. Of course, there was no guarantee she would be accepted now she had told Mavis her secrets, but this escape route was the only one she had found and its existence was the only thing providing her with a reason for living.

She had taken off her hat and replaced it with a bandanna. It enraged Howard when he saw the scar on her head so she kept it covered at all times. Now that they had stopped sharing a bed, she relished her quiet bedroom and had bought and fitted a sliding bolt at the back of the door so she could ensure her privacy for a few hours. She now slid the bolt home and turned on a bedside lamp.

The questions were not what she expected. They were far more inventive than any set of questions she had ever seen before.

What is your hidden talent?

How much furniture do you actually need?

Do you have a pet?

Are you adventurous?

What is your hobby?

Do you travel regularly, or wish to do so?

Would your close family wish to visit you?

What health issues do you have?

But the one that made her stop and think, was phrased differently from the others.

What is your Achilles heel?

She remembered the story of the Greek hero whose mother immersed him in the sacred river to protect him. She held the child by the heel of one foot as she did so, and that small place on his body became the area of his eventual downfall from a well-placed arrow.

How did this translate to Eve Dobrinski who had given her maiden name to Mavis who had trusted her? What was her weakness? Was it her inability to act to save her life?

Sitting in the bedroom where she slept alone and had a listening ear alert at all times for the heavy tread of her husband, she had to smile a thin smile, more like a grimace. Her Achilles heel was surely Howard Dobrinski, the man she had promised at the church altar to love in sickness and in health till death do us part. She had honoured that promise until she could not do it any longer.

Despite the plans to leave which she had now set in motion, she was not sure she could break the bonds of the promise and leave him forever. She felt huge guilt at even thinking of doing it. And yet, if she stayed, she knew in her innermost heart, one day Howard Dobrinski would surely kill her.

Would she wait until he made the attempt, or save herself first?

She stared at the questions without writing a word. Darkness came and the room grew cold but not as cold as her heart felt. It was a moment of decision. She felt tied to the chair until she had made the decision. It was now or never while her head was clear.

Go or stay, and suffer the consequences either way?

Go or stay?

Go or……?

Go.

Josette Delacour was happy Vilma Smith had offered to drive the Irish-sounding woman to her home, wherever that might be. She had a lot to think about after the strange meeting at Hilary's house and her car was as good a place as any for thinking. She had a quick or a slow route home and chose the latter to give her more time.

She turned the radio down low and with the background music playing she began to talk aloud.

Sacre Bleu! It really was Hilary Wilson, as I knew her then. Not aging as well as me, of course, but the same bossy personality and fussy ways. I wonder what happened to the husband? How long did he hold out before saying aurevoir forever! And who is the friend? Now she's a strange one! Staying in the background, but I could tell they were close. How close? Not much chance of coming between those two even if I wanted to....or could. The looks Hil gave me! I did not expect a kiss on the cheek but she could have spoken to me individually instead of ignoring my presence.

Do I really want to live in a house with Hilary and her partner and that Irish one and the scared little mousy one?

As for Vilma Smith....she's unusual, n'est-ce pas! There's a story there for sure. And the huge car! What a showoff!

Vraiment! the thought is not very appealing. Hil was always jealous of me. Oh yes, she was! I laughed when whatshisname, John or James something, dropped her like a hot potato when I came on the scene at school. So long ago. Like another century. Alors!, it was another century! Amazing how we are back in touch again.

I'll just bet Hil is shaking in her shoes right this minute thinking about the trouble I could cause for her.

Of course she has no idea what I really want to tell her. She'll fall off from her high horse when she finds out.

Ha! I might just stay around for a while to annoy her. It would do Henri some good to think I have a lover some-where. Serves him right for being such a tight-fisted miser.

CHAPTER 5

M avis Montgomery said goodbye to her friend Hilary and drove home. She lived on Emery Street, close to the River Thames and to downtown London, in a quaint Ontario Cottage lovingly restored by her husband Pete. There was always a sense of pleasure opening the front door and stepping inside. There was so much of Peter Montgomery here in the character touches he had added to their home. As a talented craftsman in wood and plaster, he had restored the cornices and decorative woodwork of the Gothic style and made artistic roundels on the ceilings to match photographs he found in the Central Library's archives.

She loved the home's simplicity, spacious rooms and one–and–a-half-storey plan.

What she did not love was the silence; a silence that could not be filled with music or television or occasional visits from sympathetic neighbours.

Whatever she tried, the silence was deafening.

She volunteered at the courthouse for a time, despite her retirement from there only a few years before, but found the contrast between those busy hours and the dead air in the cottage to be even more oppressive.

It was Hilary who rescued her in the end. They first met when Hilary needed advice on how to deal with a particularly recalcitrant teenager who was making her grade 8 classes a misery for their teachers.

As principal of the school, Hilary had sought help and Mavis Montgomery was recommended.

The connection between the boy's behaviour and the number of times his father had appeared in the court system soon provided Hilary with an explanation. Mavis soon devised strategies based on what she knew of the boy's home life. He had been given too many responsibilities for his younger siblings while his downtrodden mother worked every hour she could, to keep the family together during her husband's frequent jail-time absences.

Together they formed a plan. The boy was excused from some classes and given a coaching role with the physical education teacher, who was universally adored by the boys. This privilege came with responsibilities to keep the gym equipment stored properly, a task that was handed over by the teachers with the greatest relief. Finding everything in its place at the start of a lesson, accorded the boy genuine praise from the school's staff and set him on the road to success.

That boy was now a teacher himself and a star athlete of Olympic quality and it was the beginning of a long association between Mavis and Hilary that extended beyond their retirements.

Hilary's Mark died of a heart attack and Mavis and Peter stood by her until she had found her feet again.

The favour was returned after Pete fell from scaffolding on a house renovation, broke his back, and lingered in extreme pain for six long months in hospital. The friendship the two women had cherished, became something much deeper after sharing hours in Pete's hospital room and anguishing over his inevitable deterioration.

The entire period had made such a blot on Mavis's spirit that she was close to a clinical depression for many months and would have sunk beneath that mental weight had Hilary not come up with the idea of shared accommodations for mutual support and companionship.

At first, they were going to live together in Hilary's home but after much discussion, they found the house that had been adequate for one was now becoming outdated and requiring significant repairs before it would suit the two women.

Hilary made enquiries of the local real estate companies and discovered the property had grown in value because of its location near a large new downtown facility as an adjunct of a popular college.

Apparently such homes as Hilary's were needed as rental developments in which several students could share expenses while attending classes.

Hilary had an assessment done and was very pleased and surprised by the suggested selling price.

Mavis also decided to relinquish her heritage home for which there was always a market among buyers who respected the unique qualities of such rare, well-maintained buildings in good areas.

The shared home idea began to grow and shape when Mavis's home drew competition from a number of interested buyers. Hilary put her home up for private sale and together the women drew up the beginning of their plan.

The Ontario Cottage sold first. Mavis removed

her most precious personal belongings to storage and as soon as the new owners were ready to take possession she would move in with Hilary temporarily.

For now, Mavis could still appreciate her old home and love its memories without the feeling of loss. The new family would bring fresh life to this home. They adored the heritage features and could not wait for their own home in St. Mary's to be sold. They begged Mavis to sell them some of the antiques that looked perfectly in place in the cottage and she agreed to do so. It was a comfort to know Pete's work would be respected and valued into the next generations.

It was time to move on to a new phase of her life with all the excitement that created. She knew she and Hilary would manage together. They had known each other long enough to understand how to maximize the good points and minimize the lesser points of their characters. What bothered her now were the possible problems created by the new members of their co-housing plan. It had not been possible to frame a plan whereby one new person at a time could be incorporated. The large sum of money required for the future home purchase needed initial contributions. Mavis was aware this financial requirement would eliminate many women. She was surprised they had any interested parties at all and now she had seen the four women, her doubts only increased.

Hilary would have to take her concerns about the four very seriously or the plan could be in jeopardy.

Mavis knew Hilary had spent months doing a feasibility study on co-housing projects. She was a good researcher and had found a variety of sites online with advice and cautions in equal measure. She was convinced they could make this project work. Her conviction was what worried Mavis the most.

Hilary, once set on a course, was a force to be reckoned with. She was like an ocean liner that cannot be turned quickly or easily.

Mavis Montgomery acknowledged and accepted her role as the quiet voice of reason to steer toward safety whenever the ship of Hilary Dempster was venturing into dangerous waters.

The second bedroom was prepared for Mavis's eventual occupation, but Hilary took over the smallest of the three bedrooms as her office. She set up files in meticulous order with labels denoting clear headings about communal living. She found convincing arguments on both sides and maintained a running total of pros and cons. That list, pinned to a handy bulletin board was now larger than she had believed when she started out but it was almost neck and neck and that was of some concern.

"Better to have too much information," she told herself, "than not enough."

Surprisingly, she discovered this was not a new idea. The co-housing movement began in Denmark in the 1960s and there were now models in Australia and the U.K. In 2012 a California architect published a handbook on senior co-housing and in Canada there was even a Facebook page called Cohousing For Creative Aging.

Hilary pored over the various models and housing styles across Canada and found some were most focussed on developing building plans for blocks of apartment accommodation with the features of shared areas and social community. She suspected these ideas might devolve into pseudo retirement home look-alikes unless there was stringent supervision.

The sources she felt most closely mirrored her own plan, were those who advised smaller homes for no less than four, and no more than six, women.

What was common in all the advice was the urgent

need for a new way of aging in place that could cost less than the $3,000 to $4,000 a month of standard retirement facilities. Most telling was the fact that when the money ran out for these fees the residents were not guaranteed a bed. Another factor that Hilary had not previously appreciated, was that in order to enter these retirement homes, a woman had to give up most of her possessions. The rooms for residents were small to allow the space for the impressive common areas.

Co-housing benefits included many social and emotional advantages as well as the ability to retain equity in their shared home. Hilary was well aware of the legislation, municipal and provincial, that must be considered when setting up such a situation. She would need a forward-thinking lawyer to oversee contracts for each person. She had already underlined on her list the warning to be built into these contracts. As a popular Survivor television program decreed, a disagreeable resident could be 'voted off the island' by unanimous decision of the others.

As the thought struck her that it's all very well to have information, but when the theory becomes a reality and the actual persons who might be her housemates for years to come have been presented, good decisions must be made. Hilary left her desk and wandered into her bedroom where she found herself staring into the mirror behind the door.

It was past time to confront her true feelings on the matter of co-housing. It was essential to be clear on the intent and the practicalities before things progressed too far to make reversals. She straightened her broad shoulders and sucked in her stomach; a pose she had always found helpful when dealing with troublesome children or feckless parents. That added inch or two made her feel more powerful and allowed her to loom over anyone of lesser height just long enough to impress them with her capabilities. Now she lifted her strong chin and confronted her facial expression. Did she reveal uncertainty in those grey eyes? Had her mouth assumed the thin line that indicated displeasure? Was her short brown hair flopping over her eyebrows as it was wont to do in moments of stress? Was her complexion the normal shade of fading tan or was the blush of nerves highlighted her cheekbones?

She made her outer assessment and nodded approvingly at her image. Of course she could afford to lose a pound or three around her middle. Not a major concern at the moment. With the amount of work that was before her in the next few months, pounds should melt away without too much effort.

All was as it should be. Her appearance at least had passed the inspection. But what about her mental state?

She had to admit there were uncertainties in moving forward with the plan. In plain truth, it was all about choosing the right partners. One person out-of-sync with the other five might not be too much of a disruption as she would always be in the minority. But two, combining their disagreements, could be a disruptive force. She thought of the project as an orchestra in which the very different instruments were blended into a beautiful sound by the composer's musical score. Without the guiding score, the sound would be ugly and discordant. She wondered what the equivalent of a score would be in a co-housing situation. Perhaps the house rules would act as a guide for the inhabitants.

What bothered her was the thought that the orchestra analogy lacked a conductor to ensure all the musicians arrived with their instruments in the correct place and time. Was it going to be necessary to have a house mother to oversee the activities of the house partners?

If so, it would be an onerous task at best and the possibility arose of that person becoming more of a dictator. Hilary stepped away from her mirror. She knew she was the obvious choice for such a role but she also knew she was the one who would most likely act as a dictator. In her first post as principal of a school she had become so anxious for the school to be a success that she pressed too hard on her staff and caused a deputation to go above her head to the area superintendent. He was a wise man who believed in her potential and who gave her both good advice and a second chance. She never made the same mistake again and she would not do so now in far different circumstances. Hilary Dempster was content to conduct the start-up process as a 'guide on the side' but she was determined not to attempt the role of 'sage on the stage'.

At the end of her pro and con list she made the following notes:

Choose house-mates _very_ carefully.

Select a house mother even more carefully and only when absolutely necessary.

Self-determination among adults is to be preferred.

CHAPTER 6

Mavis and Hilary had prepared for the next meeting of the candidates. They had three main objectives. 1. Discuss the questionnaires.

2. Check the commitment level.

3. Answer any questions.

They waited anxiously to see who would arrive first and if all four of the women would turn up at all.

There had been no phone calls to indicate a change of mind but last minute panic was not unlikely in the circumstances.

The waiting was worse than the first time. Hilary roamed from front door to living room and made minor adjustments to the seating. They had decided to leave the dining room set up as normal with the teak table in the centre and six chairs around it. For the second meeting they would be less formal and start the discussions in the living room as if among visiting friends.

Mavis had recommended this approach.

"You should stay seated, Hilary. Read a magazine or something for now. We don't want to alarm them. I'll welcome the women as before and you start the conversation as casually as you can manage. When everyone has arrived, I will wheel in the tea trolley and we'll get down to business."

It was a fine plan but fine plans don't always turn out as expected.

Wilma Smith's car drove into the driveway at the same time as Jannice O'Connor rounded the last bend in the road. She had been running part of the way from the bus stop fearing to be late and her long black hair had been jolted free of the clasps that held it off her face and strands were now clinging to her moist forehead.

Vilma locked her car door and waited while Jannice approached at fast walking speed.

Really, she's quite a pretty little thing with that high cheek colour and the clear blue eyes. I don't think there's a vestige of makeup on her face and she looks fine. Dress her up nicely and she would be quite attractive but the clothes!! What a mess! Nothing fits her and it all must have fallen out of some old closet years ago. She needs help.

"Hi there, Jannice! What kind of week have you had? I've been clearing out my clothes and shoes all week."

"Oh, Mrs. Smith, I am so worried. You've seen where I live. I am afraid the old house will not sell for near enough cash so I can claim a place in the shared house. I will be so disappointed. This idea was my one big chance."

"Dear, dear! Please don't cry. Call me Vilma. You won't be alone to deal with this. The whole thing about living together is so we can help each other when we need help. Come inside with me and we'll see what can be done to help you."

This was the final straw. Jannice collapsed against Vilma's side in relief and wept tears of happiness.

She had twisted herself into knots for days and here was help on the very doorstep; and from such an unlikely source. Under normal circumstances she would never dream of asking a wealthy woman like Vilma Smith for assistance of any kind and now she was *offering help.*

Jannice dashed the tears from her face, tucked the errant strands of her hair back behind her ears and followed Vilma up the front steps.

It's a lesson to me, for sure. I will try never to judge a person on first impressions again.

Mavis watched this interaction through the stained glass panel on the door. She was surprised to see Vilma react with sympathy. She could not hear the words they exchanged but the body language spoke volumes. She felt sure she had an unexpected ally in Vilma and opened the door to welcome them both with real warmth.

She took their coats.

"You two are the first to arrive. The wind is chilly today and there's a definite touch of winter in the air. Hilary is in the living room waiting for you. I'll bring hot tea and coffee when everyone is here."

Next to come was Josette Delacour. She was wearing a black fur hat on her fair hair and a pair of ridiculously high heels on her feet. The heavy fur coat to match the hat was found a spot in the hall closet and Mavis felt its weight and knew it was not imitation. She thought it was risky to wear fur these days as so many people were against killing animals for this purpose. She also figured Josette probably could not care less about those opinions.

"Please go through, Josette. Vilma and Jannice have just arrived."

Hilary looked up as Josette entered and her eyes went to the shoes, as did those of Vilma and Jannice.

They had just been hearing of Vilma's attempts to clear out her shoe closet and all three could not repress a chuckle as they saw what Vilma had described as 'passion pushers' on Josette's feet.

The wearer of the shoes was not affected in the least. She presumed it was envy and as that was exactly the impression she was trying to make, she was pleased. She took a seat on the other side of the room, fluffed up her hair, smiled contentedly and made herself comfortable.

Mavis moved nervously between the front entrance and the kitchen. The trolley was ready for the boiling water to be poured into the teapot. The coffee was heating beneath the coffee maker and the cookies and scones were in place. She was beginning to fear that Eve Barton might not come today and a series of awful visions were parading through her mind. All involved actions and reactions of the husband from whom Eve had been keeping secrets. Mavis had not yet fully apprised Hilary of her worries about Eve. She knew that discussion could not be postponed much longer. She was waiting to see what today's meeting would reveal.

Just as she was adding more napkins to the trolley, she heard a quiet tap on the front door. She saw the familiar slouchy hat and the awkward angle of head she recognized from their first meeting and opened the door quickly before anyone else noticed. The volume of voices in the living room should give them a moment or two of private conversation.

"Eve, I am so glad to see you. Come inside out of the wind. Did you come by cab again? How are you?

Sorry! I am not giving you a chance to reply. I have been anxious about you."

"I am here safely, Mavis, and that's all that is important for now. It's most kind of you to be concerned for me and I appreciate it more than you can know. I am looking forward to today's discussion. I have my answers ready. I hope they will suffice."

"Don't worry. Come in and take a seat. Keep your hat on as before, if you wish. Give me a hand with the trolley."

Hilary looked up as the two women pushed the trolley forward into the room.

"Excellent! Everyone is here. Help yourselves to a hot drink and something sweet. Mavis's raisin and cheese scones are legendary. She brought extras."

Eve clutched her questionnaire in her hand and sat down. Mavis poured a cup of tea for her and balanced a fudge cookie on the saucer. "I think you took milk the last time, Eve. Relax for a minute. We'll start soon."

Eve nodded gratefully. She felt inadequate to

enter the conversations of the others and needed space to calm her beating heart.

Hilary waited until everyone was served then she commenced on the program they had decided upon. First, she announced that the questionnaires would not be collected.

"I imagine you guessed I was a teacher for some years but this is not an exam. The purpose of Mavis's questions is to give you a chance to think more deeply about the shared house idea."

There was an outbreak of relieved laughter in the room. Four women visibly relaxed and the questions began at once with a comment.

"I found these questions to be thought-provoking and I'm sure I was not alone in that."

Hilary immediately noticed how Vilma had included the others in her comment. This was a good sign and a point in her favour. She was not the superficial rich woman she first appeared to be.

Jannice smiled at Vilma and ventured to add, "I thought a lot about all the questions and the one I want to mention is about hidden talents. You see I'm afraid I don't have much to offer in the other categories and I am not sure I will be included in this wonderful plan in the end, but I do have practical nursing skills. I looked after both my parents at home until they died and there's not much I haven't seen or done in that department. I am also willing to act in any other helpful capacity, if needed."

Jannice visibly deflated after this long speech. It was as if she had summoned up everything in her and now she was emptied out.

Mavis, who had seen her distraught arrival at the house only a few minutes previously, was impressed by her courage and quick to respond. "Thank you, Jannice. Those are very important suggestions. Does anyone have anything to add on the issue of hidden talents?"

Attention now moved to the others and Jannice cast a grateful glance toward Mavis.

Josette decided she needed to divert interest away from these women she considered to be born losers.

"Well, personally, I have many talents, none of them hidden." She chuckled knowingly at this jest. "However, I am more concerned about comforts and facilities like square footage and private bathrooms and space for cars. *Comprenez-vous?*

Mavis let Hilary handle this one. She was becoming more and more convinced that Josette was not going to be a compatible companion for this venture.

"Yes, Jo. These concerns are valid, of course, but we are still a long way from decisions like that. If and when we choose our house we can get into specifics."

Hilary's tone was cool and Josette was delighted to have thrown a spanner into the works as it were. She settled back in her chair and watched with interest to see what would emerge next.

Surprisingly, to both Hilary and Mavis, it was Eve Barton who spoke up. She pulled nervously at her hat and swallowed visibly.

"I agree it's early days to be talking about details but I need to know now when I can submit my fee. I am not a financial expert, although I did an accountancy degree years ago. I believe a large sum of money can be placed in a safe investment and the interest accumulated to benefit everyone involved. Would this not be a good idea?"

Mavis knew at once this inquiry came from Eve's need to move her inherited money away from her husband's grasp as soon as possible. She signalled to Hilary that she would respond and did so quickly.

"Of course, you are right, Eve. Such an investment could be important for us and it is something to consider seriously. Today we really want to hear about issues such as family, pets and other requirements to guide our future decisions. May I talk to you privately later about your idea?"

Eve nodded and subsided into her chair. Mavis knew she would not likely speak up again.

Once more Vilma filled the uncomfortably gap.

"I have no family to speak of, so that does not concern me, but I have always wanted to have a dog. Don't they say a dog is a great companion and also a way to integrate into a new neighbourhood? What do others think about it?"

The atmosphere lightened up. "I have a cat," said Mavis. "She's a quiet little animal and I hope to keep her. I believe we can establish rules for pets and their owners and I agree with Vilma's beliefs. Pets are good for mental health in many ways."

"What?" exploded Josette. "You can't have animals if people have allergies. I hate animals of all kinds and I would not want their hairs and nasty habits to be part of my home. A vote is required on this and other debatable points."

Here we go again! Hilary was rapidly losing patience with her old enemy but glad she was revealing her true nature this soon.

"No decisions yet, Josette. I will make a note about your concerns.

Now, what about travel? Is anyone likely to want to flee the winter for Florida or other warm spots?"

The conversation turned to happier topics and Vilma offered the option of sharing a property she had acquired from her first husband in a rental building on the beach in Jamaica.

"There's an agency to look after rentals for me. It's a nice bit of income and a week is always reserved for my occupancy in February."

"Sure now, and why wouldn't you be wanting to stay there permanently?" asked Jannice. Jamaica in the winter sounded like paradise to her.

"Well, it's nice to get some sun but the tourist population changes so much, it's difficult to form friendships. I want to have a home where I am assured of companionship in a safe country with many amenities close by."

Casual conversation continued after this. Fresh hot drinks were poured and soon Hilary was looking at her watch. Mavis had retreated to the kitchen with Eve Barton for a quick conference. She informed her that there was a bank account already set up into which she and Hilary would deposit their sums of money as soon as their houses were sold.

"I would not announce this to the others. It's too soon, but I want you to know, Eve, you could transfer your money there if you are really sure you want to risk it this early in the process. Also, I must now make it clear to Hilary how your situation might impact our future plans."

"I trust you, Mavis. I have since the first minute. I

can't ask anyone else to help me. It's too dangerous. Howard might retaliate if he knew the person. Anonymity is my only hope.

If I can escape my present situation I would love to live with you and whomever you choose to join you.

If you are willing, I will bring the cash sum with me to our next meeting and leave it in your hands.

Please consider it."

"If you are this concerned for your safety, Eve, go ahead and bring the cash with you. I realize I can't call you at home but promise me you will be careful and come here quickly in a cab as soon as you have the money. I appreciate your confidence in us. The last thing you want is to be cheated of this inheritance and whatever freedom it can buy for you."

Eve closed her eyes for a moment. When she opened them she looked at Mavis Montgomery and saw, not the ordinary woman with delicate features and green eyes behind gold-rimmed glasses, but an angelic figure whose hands had reached out to grasp hers with a friendship and comfort Eve had never been able to claim in her whole life. Whatever happened from this point on she felt she would be safe and secure.

"There you are, Mavis! I am just about to bring this session to a close. Come and join us, Eve."

The date for the next meeting, a week ahead, was announced, and the women made their way to the hall closet in a flurry of talk that was entirely different from the previous week's silences.

Hilary stood back. She had collected phone and email information from the women, except from Eve Barton. There was something going on there between Eve and Mavis. She would get to the bottom of it as soon as the house had cleared.

She had promised to inform all the candidates by phone of their decision within a few days. It would be a most important discussion with Mavis and it had to start now.

CHAPTER 7

Vilma drove Jannice O'Connor home once again but on this occasion she stopped the car and asked Jannice to describe the situation inside her home that was giving her the impression she could not meet the financial requirements.

"Well, you can see the condition of the houses here. It's not a desirable area at the moment. I don't think the house would fetch more than a hundred thousand and that's if it was in much better shape than it is presently."

"So, what is wrong with the condition? ….and just tell me the truth Jannice. I can't help if I don't know the situation."

Jannice lowered her gaze to her feet then breathed in and gathered her courage.

"It's a mess! There's junk piled in most of the rooms. Nothing has been done to update the place for decades and it's ugly as sin. I blame myself. I have done nothing about this state of affairs since my mother's passing and now it's impossible."

"But you want to move to the shared house, don't you? Then you have to pull up your socks, my girl, and get moving. You are not working outside the home so start cleaning up right away. We can make an appointment with those 'Got Junk' people to take away what you don't need and then we can see if there's anything worth selling. If the house has been untouched for as long as you suggest there may be antiques or something valuable in there. Give it a try. I'll call you tomorrow for a progress report and I hope you will have plenty to tell me."

Jannice was shocked. No one cared enough about her predicament to give advice or hope. She had none of her own. Now, both advice and hope were being dispensed by the same amazing woman who was so far out of her class that Jannice would never expect her to give a damn at all.

The shock was doing strange things to her. A current of energy or panic, she could not tell which, was racing through her body from top to toe and she felt as if she could do anything. This feeling was unlikely to last but she began to believe she could actually do as Vilma said. She could make a start.

Her head came up and she looked Vilma Smith straight in the eye for the first time.

"Thank you. You are a real motivator. I will do it. I will start right now. Thank you."

Before Vilma could react to being called a motivator for the first time in her life, Jannice was out of the car and marching up the short walk with a purposeful step and keys in her hand.

Well now! That was a surprise. I was thinking I had gone too far but it looks as if it was exactly what the poor woman needed. A pity I never got such a positive response when I told my stepdaughters to clean up their rooms!

Vilma took off the hand brake and set the window wipers going. She had begun to tackle the shoe closet at her own, for now, home, but there was more to be done. She needed to practise what she was preaching and set to the task of sorting through her correspondence and other papers. She had no intention of leaving one single piece of private paper for those vultures to paw over.

It's a nasty wet day, I may as well do something useful and I will be able to tell Jannice about my progress.

Before Vilma's car had left the street, Jannice had her coat off and her sleeves rolled up. She stood for a moment contemplating which room would show the most improvement and thereby encourage her to keep going. She decided to start in the kitchen where there was a small area of clear countertop holding an electric kettle, a toaster and the one plate, mug and bowl with the cutlery she used and washed each day. A small pot for boiling an egg or heating soup and a frying pan, for occasional more ambitious meals, were there also.

The rest of the kitchen which occupied the back half of the long, narrow terraced house lay untouched and now that she looked at it more closely she could see dust on open shelves and what looked suspiciously like a spider web hanging from the upper cupboards. She went downstairs to the basement laundry room to fetch baskets. For years she had ignored the accumulated junk down here and kept a pathway to the washer and dryer cleared for her use. Now her eyes were opened she sighed, but kept her resolve. She would make a start as she had promised Vilma. She would not allow herself to be discouraged.

Two hours went by and contrary to her expectations, Jannice felt more energy as she progressed through the cupboards throwing anything broken, chipped or stained beyond help into one basket, and selecting anything that might have value to be layered in the other with hand towels and dishtowels she discovered in a plastic box in a lower cupboard she had never before opened.

Inspired by initial success, she continued to open up cupboards, some of which were almost stuck together with years of grime and neglect. Inside one she found a jumbled pile of blackened metal objects which she eventually figured out to be tarnished silver, long left unpolished. She placed these into a plastic bin bag for later consideration and moved on.

On a high shelf with a grimy glass front she spied something with a lace edge and after standing on a chair for a closer look it turned out to be one of a collection of delicate hand-made and hand-embroidered linen cloths. She presumed these were possessions of a grandmother she had never met who was the first owner of the house in a previous century. The stitched-on labels had the name Sinead O'Connor in fine thread. She handled them with care, grateful they had been protected from damage by the clear plastic box.

This discovery gave her pause for thought and she stopped to make tea. Sitting at the battered kitchen table she looked around her with a different pair of eyes. Were there any other items surviving from the era of Sinead, her grandmother or great-grandmother? This brought a new perspective to the work. Instead of a burdensome chore she had ignored for decades while her parents were so ill, the task began to take on the feel of a treasure hunt. At least, she might uncover more about family members she should have known. The stressful years of caring for invalids and dealing with the meagre home care hours she was allocated, had not allowed for long pleasant reminiscences about earlier times.

She regretted the lost opportunities now but here was the chance to attempt to find out more on her own. Perhaps there might be other named items she could trace. There might even be family members, descendants somewhere, who could be contacted.

As she considered this new idea, it arrived with the comforting thought that she might not be totally alone in the world. For certain sure, she had Vilma Smith as her champion and who knew who else might be uncovered from a dusty, dingy past?

The tea cup was empty. She selected a set for one, of an elaborate china tea service she had found and placed the old plain set in the reject basket. From now on Jannice Erin O'Connor would live with the best around her. Now that she had tackled the kitchen cupboards with some success, she would move on to the bathroom cupboards and clear out the expired medications that lingered there.

It would truly be a clean sweep.

~

Mavis and Hilary exchanged glances as soon as they had closed the door on their last guest.

"Well, that was revealing, don't you agree? Vilma Smith is impressive, I thought."

"I do agree and we must compare notes about the others at once before the details escape us."

They soon assembled in their favourite place for discussions, the island countertop in the bright, airy kitchen. Hilary made fresh coffee in the Keurig machine and they both inhaled the fragrance in their cups before adding milk or cream.

"You start first, Mavis. I suspect you have more to say."

Mavis sipped thoughtfully and reached for a chocolate biscuit for added strength.

"I have two things to say. First, I dislike your old friend Josette and I hope that does not offend you."

"Quite the contrary! She was never a friend, more of a school-days' acquaintance, if that, and I believe she showed her true colours today. I vote to reject her application and we can discuss what the implications are of that act later, all right?"

Mavis was relieved. *Now to tackle the thorny subject of one Eve Barton.*

"I mentioned before that Eve Barton was likely to

be problematic. I do not deny the problems which I will outline for you at once, but I must preface my remarks with a plea for leniency."

"Goodness sake, Mavis Montgomery! You are not in the courthouse now. I am more than willing to hear you out without criticizing. You know how much I value your opinion."

"Thank you, Hilary. That is kind of you, but I do feel as if I need to be an advocate on Eve's behalf. You see, she is all alone in her situation. Her husband is an abuser and she is afraid of him and what he might do if she attempts to escape him. She wants to disappear in such a way that he cannot track her down. You heard her question about depositing her portion of the house purchase money? Well, she is anxious to put it somewhere safe before her husband, Howard, can take it from her."

"This is a dire business, Mavis. I can see why you feel you need to help this woman but we could be in the middle of a legal nightmare if this Howard gets wind of her location with us."

"I've been thinking about that part. Eve told me she has been using her maiden name and she doesn't want to tell me her married name for now. I think she first has to feel secure that we won't betray her.

If this Howard is unlikely to report her absence because of his alcoholic and wife-battering habits, it could be possible Eve would be able to disappear at least until she has recovered from her fear."

"It seems as if this money is a godsend for the poor woman. How did it happen?"

"I'm not sure. I imagine it must be from an unlikely source or her husband would already have some knowledge of it."

There was silence in the kitchen, other than the sound of cups touching the countertop. Mavis watched her friend's face for clues on her decision but could detect nothing. Hilary had the ability to conceal her feelings. Something she claimed she had found useful during her teaching years and which was now automatic.

Mavis could no longer abide the tension.

"What do you think Hilary? Can we take the risk?"

"I do sympathize with Eve, and with your good-hearted tendency to help the downtrodden."

Mavis tensed waiting for a 'but'. The silence returned until Hilary took a deep breath then let it out all at once.

"When we decided to begin on this project we promised each other a new start in life and to welcome any adventures that might come our way. Eve Barton is not exactly what we had in mind then, but she does represent both a new start and an adventure of a kind, I suppose. We can hardly turn her away now. There is one thing we must be sensitive to, Mavis. We are entering a conspiracy and we will have to judge carefully which, if any, of our partners should be party to the conspiracy. A wrong word to the wrong person could bring this Howard to our door with dangerous consequences."

"Of course you are right about that, Hilary. It's an important consideration."

She paused to let the thought fold into her mental picture. It was a bold decision for a woman like Hilary to take. It would be up to Mavis to make certain it was a good one for all the partners.

"May I tell Eve next week we are willing to go ahead?"

"Yes. We can accept her financial contribution into our designated bank account and provide a receipt until we get the contracts drawn up. We are only at the beginning of this journey and things could change before we reach the point of setting up home together."

"I accept that proviso, Hilary. We'll see what develops and act cautiously in the meantime."

She lifted her cup and indicated a toast was required now that the decision had been made. Hilary responded with a smile and the comment that she would be responsible for delivering the bad news to Josette by phone.

"It leaves us one house member short but the ad cards are still in place and someone may turn up."

With that, they returned to their respective tasks for the day. Hilary in the upstairs office and Mavis to return home to look over her clothes and see if there was something more she could recycle now that Vilma Smith had raised the style standards.

CHAPTER 8

Only two weeks after the first meeting, the pace of events acquired a forward motion of its own and began to accelerate.

Hilary had called Vilma and Jannice with the news they were accepted as house partners if they so wished. Vilma was not surprised, but Jannice declared she was more than willing to participate but there was some doubt regarding the financial side of things.

"There's a long way to go before we need to make the deposit, Jannice. Several of us have houses to sell. All of it will take time. If necessary, we can help with finances. You have already shown your willingness to take on added responsibilities and that will be taken into account."

The next call had been left to the end so that Hilary could summon up courage. She reached the number Josette had left and was surprised to hear a male voice on the end of the line.

"Jo isn't here right now. Who's calling? I'll pass on the message."

It was a brief encounter but enough to consolidate Hilary's feeling about Josette's unsuitability for the shared home. Clearly she had lied about her circumstances. It was not unlikely she was living with a man. Josette Delacour was not the type of woman to live long without a male companion on the scene.

Now Hilary wondered why on earth Jo had thought she was suitable for the project in the first place.

She did not have long to wait to find out.

The phone rang late in the evening. In the office where she was finishing her paperwork, Hilary picked up the phone on the second ring somewhat annoyed at being disturbed.

"Hilary? You called earlier?"

"I did, Josette. I am sorry to tell you we have decided not to accept your application for a place in our future co-housing project."

There was an intake of breath on the line then silence for several heartbeats until a raucous laugh assaulted Hilary's eardrum.

"Alors! This is a surprise, Hil. I did not think you had the guts to make such a decision. I was not serious about your little project. It's nothing to me to be excluded."

"Why did you respond to the advert?"

"Oh it was just a notion I had to see how you had survived the years."

"You could have simply called me for that. Why the elaborate subterfuge?"

Another explosive laugh caused Hilary to momentarily pull the phone away from her ear.

"What a word to use, Hil, but then you always were a stuck-up, supercilious madam."

"I think this conversation is at an end. Goodbye."

"No, wait just one moment. I have an important piece of information you must hear."

"What is it? I am rapidly losing patience with you, Josette."

"Well, someone you know had a lot of patience with me; your husband Mark, for instance? Such a good lover, n'est-ce pas? He cheated on you for months while you were doing your principal's courses, or something of the kind. He felt so neglected and I gave him comfort. We......"

The phone fell from her hands and hit the leg of the desk on the way down. She could not breathe.

Her chest had constricted with anguish, shock and pain. Thoughts and memories flooded her mind. The only time she and Mark had fought endlessly over anything at all was her decision to advance her career. She elected to take the courses in the States one summer, despite his objections. It was weeks before things went back to normal again.

A sudden rush of pure anger made her able to draw breath again. She expected nothing good of Josette Delacour. But Mark? He was a man of honour, or so she had believed. If she could have him here in front of her for one second she would land him such a blow he would fly into tomorrow.

This image made her stop and think. It was ludicrous to imagine such a scene. Mark was gone. Jo was a nonentity and she might well be lying in order to hurt Hilary. She was a jealous bitch who always stole men from other girls.

The thought occurred that she could call Jo's husband? man friend? and reveal things about his partner that would curl his hair, but that would be descending to Jo's level, something Hilary Dempster could not contemplate.

She decided to go to bed, read her spy novel until her mind was wiped clean of the base accusations and never ever mention one word of the nasty conversation to a living soul. Good riddance!

~

On the morning of the third meeting at Hilary's house, Mavis took a call in the kitchen where she was preparing sandwiches. She suspected the group would need sustenance now that things were solidified with regard to future intentions. It was likely to be a longer meeting.

"Good morning. Can I help you?"

"I believe so."

The voice was deep and pleasant with a light air of humour about it. Mavis knew it was not the voice of one of the women she was expecting to hear from.

"You see, I have been very busy lately and I have missed the first meetings regarding the shared housing project. Is it at all possible for me to join the group at this late date?"

"Ah, may I have your name?"

"It's Honor Pace. I had every intention of coming in November but my plans were changed at the last minute and I could not do anything about it."

"Well, Miss Pace, it just so happens that we are having our third meeting today. If you have the original ad please come along. Same place, same time. You can meet everyone and see how you feel."

"That is wonderful. Thank you so much. I will

see you later then. Am I speaking to Miss Dempster, or to Miss Montgomery?"

"This is Mavis Montgomery. I am making sandwiches for the meeting. Bring your appetite."

"I will do that."

Mavis went straight to the office to find Hilary.

"We will need a new card, my dear. Remember Honor Pace? She wants to come today."

"Well now, that's a surprise. What delayed her?

"I really don't know but I have a good feeling about her, based on our conversation on the phone. We'll find out more later."

It was a good start to the day but things changed as the hours went on.

Vilma Smith and Jannice O'Connor arrived together. They were chatting away like old friends about something related to dishes, as far as Mavis could discern. The other notable item was Jannice's appearance. Her long dark hair was swept back and up, in what looked like a French roll. A silver pin held the style in place and the ill-fitting clothes were gone replaced by a bright red, three-quarter length lined raincoat and a pair of slim black pants over black leather boots.

"You two look ready for the day!"

"I have Vilma to thank for this." Jannice swirled around to show off her outfit like a young girl in a party dress. "She found some clothes in her own closet and brought them for me. We had quite a fashion show. It was wonderful!"

Jannice's enthusiasm brought a warm glow to her cheeks. The new clothes had transformed her from a weary middle-aged woman into a younger, happier version of herself.

Mavis signalled a 'well done' toward Vilma who was watching this exchange with a proud look on her smiling face. Mavis thought it was a shame the children of her husband had not taken the opportunity to allow this side of Vilma Smith to emerge.

Jannice was almost reluctant to relinquish her red coat to the hall closet but underneath it she had a very pretty blue blouse that complemented her eyes perfectly.

What an unlikely couple, but how marvellous to see real benefits between house partners so soon.

Hilary was waiting in the kitchen and soon caught up with the excitement of the first arrivals. She seemed relieved that Josette was gone and anxious to meet the new candidate.

Honor Pace emerged from a cab just five minutes later. Mavis opened the door and saw immediately that she was using a sturdy stick. Mavis went out to assist her by taking her free arm. She was rewarded with a warm smile and explanations began at once.

"I have arthritis. I missed the meetings because I was confined to hospital for a hip replacement after an accident. Physiotherapy has been helping me but I did not want to risk coming out until I could handle the stick with more ease."

Mavis could feel how much weight was on her arm as they slowly climbed the front steps. Honor was not a slender woman. She had a young face and her mop of thick short hair was dyed a vivid red.

"Let's find you a comfortable chair and something hot to drink. Have you come far?"

"No. I live in an apartment building in Cherryhill Village but my circumstances mean I am isolated for most of the time. That's why I responded to your advert."

They bypassed the kitchen and settled Honor in a high-backed Lazy-Boy chair formerly used by Mark Dempster.

Hilary had seen them in the front hall and came at once to meet the newcomer.

"Hello Honor. I am Hilary and so pleased to welcome you. You could not have known, but today's topic of discussion is health requirements. Two other members of our group are coming to meet you also. I hope you will become one of our partners in this co-housing project."

General conversation filled the next ten minutes.

After that Hilary became nervous and Mavis knew why. There was no sign of Eve Barton. No contact from her all week was not unusual in her circumstances but for her to miss a meeting was worrying.

Finally, Hilary went ahead with the first question while Mavis hovered nervously between the living room and the front door. She could hear Hilary's voice.

"Can we think ahead for a moment? Add ten years and tell me what you might expect from your surroundings to accommodate your independent living needs."

Jannice spoke up. "As you know, I watched my parents through their declining years. They were reasonably active for quite a long time before their health failed. My father was a lifelong smoker and his lungs eventually grew very weak. Emphysema claimed him in the end. My mother worked for a construction company supervising new buildings in old parts of the city. She was injured in an industrial accident and died later on from complications."

She rushed on with a confidence that appeared new to some of her listeners.

"The point I am trying to make is that it's difficult to look far ahead. Sometimes a small problem becomes bigger when we age and sometimes a situation long in the making arrives with devastating impact."

No one could deny Jannice's summary. She had the experience of caring for her elders while both Mavis and Hilary had cared for ailing husbands. Health issues were unpredictable as Jannice so rightly stated.

Honor Pace spoke up in the thoughtful silence that followed Jannice's story.

"I understand what this young lady just said. I was not bothered by my arthritis as a teenager. In my twenties I noticed a few small problems but it was not until my thirties that symptoms became troublesome. I will likely need a second hip operation. If I am interpreting your question correctly, Hilary, I, for one, would require a way to move from floor to floor in a regular house without having to climb stairs. I work from home and need a room large enough for both sleeping and working. I must also add that I have confidence I will be perfectly mobile once this hip has healed. I am thinking ahead as you asked."

"Exactly! Now, finding a house for six with a stair lift would be difficult but one of our ideas was to convert a series of aligned cupboards to install a lift. This would avoid later problems for all of us. What else do you think we could need?"

"I think sufficient washrooms are a necessity," added Mavis." My bladder is not what it was and I prefer a facility on each level of a house."

There was laughter as each woman sympathized with this confession.

"Extra washrooms can be an expensive option but I see heads nodding in support of Mavis. You can all see why we require such a large sum of money. We must think ahead and alter our home at the beginning so later issues do not catch us off guard."

Hilary was soon compiling a list of possible amendments.

Mavis went back to the front door to see if Eve was walking along the street toward 46 Camden Corners but there was no sign of her. She began to worry seriously. Anything could have happened to Eve. She was vulnerable and alone. Mavis had no address for her and she did not know her real last name. All she had were three photographs taken quickly and privately at last week's meeting. One was of her head wearing the slouch hat and two were of her face and head showing the bruises and the livid scar the hat concealed.

Because of her courthouse work, she knew the importance of evidence. Eve was initially reluctant to provide this evidence, but Mavis persuaded her to allow it as a precaution against her husband's future actions should he trace her to the new location.

She doubted these photos were sufficient to identify Eve to police and she did not want to set in motion an investigation. Yet, every minute lost could be fatal for Eve.

She searched her memory for a useful clue and came up with the name of Eve's bank where she had deposited the inheritance cheque.

As soon as the house emptied Mavis got into her car and drove to the bank with no clear idea of what she would do there. When she parked in the mall parking she realized the folly of her mission. It was impelled by panic. It was the only thing she could think of to do.

She was here now and might as well step inside. The bank was busy and there was a hum of activity. She stood by the doors and looked around help-lessly. She could not even enquire. Tellers would not give her private customer information. She had only a first name and even that might be false. She turned to leave when her eye caught sight of a familiar brown item on the floor under a chair. Immediately she knew it was Eve's hat. She retrieved it and went to the nearby receptionist's desk with the hat in her hand.

"Excuse me. Have you seen the woman who owns this hat? I was to meet her here."

"Oh my! I am so sorry. Let me get a manager to speak to you. Please wait for one moment."

This was confusing, but Mavis waited. Glances were being thrown her way and tellers seemed to be whispering about her. She did not hold out much hope of receiving useful information about Eve but something must have happened here.

A female manager with a name pin on her lapel ushered Mavis into her office and asked her to sit.

"I understand you know Eve Dobrinski?"

"Well, I know her as Eve Barton."

Might as well tell the truth as much as possible.

"Yes, that is her maiden name. I am so sorry to inform you that Eve collapsed here in the bank about forty minutes ago."

Mavis did not have to feign shock. She took in a shallow breath and felt blood drain from her face.

"What on earth happened?"

"As far as I know, she was waiting to see me. I handle her banking needs. She suddenly fell to the floor and did not regain consciousness. Naturally, we called for an ambulance and they took her away. We haven't heard anything since then. It's been very upsetting."

Mavis's brain was racing. "Do you know which hospital they were heading to?"

"I heard one of the paramedics say LHSC Emergency just after I had told them what little I know about Eve. Do you want to leave your contact information in case we need to speak to you?"

"I'll be in touch. Right now I need to find out how Eve is."

"Of course! Please tell her Sue is asking for her."

Mavis was back in her car in seconds and heading for the hospital. She still had Eve's hat in her hand. The paramedics must have seen her scar at once. They would suspect head trauma and take her straight into Emergency for treatment. She would enquire but she might have to wait for hours. At least she had the correct name now. Or both names, if required.

First she would call Hilary and bring her into the picture. Then she would start searching the online phone book for Dobrinski. She knew Eve lived close to a strip mall in the city. She also knew Eve's husband worked as a mechanic. She might even see him arrive at the hospital to enquire about his wife although what that confrontation would feel like when she reacted to his treatment of Eve, was an unknown at the moment.

She was pretty sure Hilary would not approve of her actions but fear for Eve was predominant.

Until she knew she was safe, she would wait at the hospital.

CHAPTER 9

Honor Pace allowed the cab driver to help her into her apartment building. She gave him a nice tip for this service and he wished her a good day. In the elevator she leaned against the wall and decided it was a good day, despite the discomfort of her hip and the inconvenience of low-slung cabs and houses with steps at the entrance. That Mavis lady was very kind and Hilary seemed organized and knowledgeable. The prospect of moving into a home with these four women was promising so far.

Making her way slowly three doors along from the elevator on the third floor, she gladly sank into a chair in her small apartment and placed her right leg up onto a padded bench. She had physio exercises to do later but for now she needed to rest.

The hip operation had given her a chance to stop and think about her future. Working from home as a computer expert was a given. It was a guaranteed income and she had clients who valued her skills highly, as proved by their bonus fees whenever she solved their technology problems. For years she had saved money. When mobility is an issue, you don't have reasons to move around too much. Others might have bought a town house or condo of some kind but whenever she looked online the huge variety of such types almost always had barriers to free access, despite regulations to the contrary.

She had tried ground level apartments with quick access to the street level but those places were easy targets for break-ins and she feared she might not be able to flee fast enough to avoid injury.

The physiotherapist in the hospital was a kind and concerned woman who listened to Honor and was willing to give her opinion on health as well as safety. She recommended more gentle exercise. Sitting at a desk all day was not helping to maintain flexibility. She gave Honor the chance to try a standing desk set up where she could walk on a treadmill while working at a fixed counter that she could angle to suit her needs. This seemed radical at first but Honor was getting the message she could no longer continue with the bad habits that had brought her to the point of a hip operation. Changes had to be made.

The physiotherapist gently introduced the topic of companionship after hearing that her patient had no family living in the London area and few if any friends to call upon in an emergency.

"Look, it's none of my business but I think you would benefit from having like-minded people around you for support. Good health is not just physical. We need daily contact with others to keep us mentally healthy."

"Hold on! I am way too young for one of those retirement places with wheelchairs and scheduled happy hours. That would spell death to me."

"No! I am thinking of a different lifestyle choice, perhaps sharing accommodation or inviting someone to live with you. Give it some thought. We all have to make compromises sooner or later."

The words had stuck with her. Then there was the ad in the grocery store followed by the fall on a wet floor, the hip operation and the recovery period.

Finally she had taken action. Today's visit to Hilary's home made the prospect of co-housing seem achievable. There was a long way to go before it was a reality. The women she met had property to sell while Honor was ready now. She would continue to keep in touch and do everything possible to regain her strength. She expected a settlement from the fall on wet pavement in the mall, and her savings would fill in the gap until she needed to cash in some of her investments. One of the advantages to working with astute business people was hearing about reliable investment companies with excellent records for paying out high dividend yields.

Honor Pace glanced out the window at the snow beginning to fall. With any luck, by spring she would be in a far different environment, surrounded by women who would provide stimulating companionship and added security. For now, she would make a meal and review her stocks and shares before starting on her exercises.

Her life was about to change for the better and she was determined to be ready.

~

Mavis had approached the Reception area behind a Perspex screen and asked for information about her 'cousin' Eve Barton. The woman consulted a screen and typed for a minute before stating she had no patient in Emergency under that name.

"She might have been registered under Eve

Dobrinski, her married name? She came by ambulance."

A few more nerve-wracking seconds and the reply was more positive.

"Yes, she has been admitted and is under medical care at the moment. It seems it has been difficult to find her information. Do you wish to register as next-of-kin? Fill out this form. She is still unconscious. I'll inform the doctor you are here. Please take a seat."

The minutes ticked by and the waiting room filled up with an assortment of distressed people. Only a few were called for consultation. The remainder waited impatiently and Mavis heard the distant screech of ambulances approaching the hospital entrance. The man seated next to her said it was always like this when the first snow of the winter fell.

"The idiots forget how to drive in snow and zoom all over the road without control. My brother was hit at the bus stop. He likely has a broken leg."

Mavis said a few words of sympathy then resumed her watch on the door to the Emergency section.

No one could enter there without permission. The reception desk nurses had control of a switch which caused the double doors to open. Mavis had a quick glimpse of a long corridor inside and hospital personnel moving from place to place at a leisurely pace. There were no patients to be seen.

After what seemed like an hour, a male doctor emerged and called her name. The man sitting beside her muttered 'Good luck!' as Mavis jumped up and walked toward the doors.

A young doctor was waiting for her.

"I understand you are related to our patient Eve Dobrinski?"

She nodded and followed along as they passed entrances to areas where some beds were concealed behind curtains.

"Mrs. Dobrinski has not regained consciousness and we have no contact information. She has only a bank book in her possession and the address is obscured. Perhaps you can help."

"Yes, of course. Doctor, what is wrong with Eve?"

"We'll know better when she can speak but it looks like she has had trauma to the head and a blood clot has shifted suddenly and is pressing on the nerves causing her collapse. We may need to remove the pressure but hopefully she will respond soon. Talk to her."

He swept aside a green curtain and Mavis saw Eve, propped up on pillows and with closed eyes in a pale face. There was a new scar on her head that appeared to be close to the former injury.

"Oh, Eve, my dear. It's Mavis. I've come to help you. Please wake up. I promise to take care of you."

She picked up the limp hands folded over her stomach and gently massaged them while murmuring consoling words. There was a tiny flicker of an eyelid just as another person pushed back the curtain and asked if she could enter. This older woman had a badge stating she was a social worker.

Mavis immediately found herself in a dilemma. She knew the home situation of Eve. Could she reveal it now, knowing well what would result once the officials were involved; investigations, inspections, interviews with Eve's husband and possibly dragging Hilary into the mix.

And yet, she could not lie. The time when Mavis Montgomery could secretly protect Eve Barton had passed.

On observing the doubt on Mavis's face, the social worker quietly continued.

"You see, Eve has some bruising as well as the head injuries. We are required to find out if she has been abused in any way. Can you advise us at all?"

Mavis stood and motioned that they should go into the common area together. She quickly explained her knowledge of the home situation and indicated her expertise in such cases based on her courthouse experience. She said she had not known Eve long but she had no reason to doubt that her husband, Howard, had inflicted the injuries.

"I won't go into the circumstances under which I met Eve but you do need to know I have a safe place for her to go to when she recovers. She should be among friends as I'm sure you can understand. Here's my information. Contact me at any time and know this. Eve is mortally afraid of her husband. She should not be left alone with him if he turns up at the hospital."

As she finished speaking, Mavis heard a small sound from the hospital bed. She rushed back inside and found Eve struggling to sit up. She spoke reassuringly to her while the social worker went to fetch the doctor.

A few quick tests with a light pen assured the doctor there was no lasting damage in the brain.

"We will keep you under observation for a day or two to make sure the swelling that caused you to collapse is under control. I'll arrange a bed for you. Your friend can call or visit once you are settled in. Don't worry. We'll look after you now."

His final words affected Eve. Mavis saw the relief on her face.

Poor woman. She's been living in fear for so long that even a hospital is like a sanctuary to her.

"I was going to collect my money from the bank and bring it to you for safekeeping, Mavis,' she whispered." I don't know what happened or how you got here but I am so glad to see you."

"Just sit back and relax, Eve. I have spoken to the social worker. She knows your situation. They will interview your husband but you need not see him again if that is what you wish. Your first priority is to get well. After that we'll settle everything else. Trust me."

Eve closed her eyes and sank back into the pillows. Exhaustion was sweeping over her.

Mavis waited till her breathing was regular and some colour had returned to her face. She tiptoed out and walked slowly back to the double-door exit. She pushed a round metal button to the side and the doors opened outward. Escape!

The entire experience had thrust her back to her working days at the London courthouse. The barely concealed air of panic in the waiting room, the questions and concerns of the medical personnel and the knowledge of life and death decisions being made all around you were familiar reminders of the highly-charged atmosphere in the courts of law.

She shook it all off as she inhaled the crisp, cold

air. Snow was falling and she had forgotten where she parked the car. Scrabbling in her pocket, she found the parking ticket stamped Emergency Priority Parking and headed uphill toward the entrance. She would pay by credit card as she had no idea how long she had spent in the hospital.

Next would come the explanations for Hilary. She hoped that lady was in a good humour.

When Mavis drew into the parking space at Camden Corners the windshield wipers had been swishing back and forth for some time as the snowfall developed. She had driven slowly and carefully, mindful of the man in the waiting room's comments about the first snow.

As she climbed the front steps, she was overcome with exhaustion. She had kept her energy levels up all through the hospital experience but now she saw safety, she let go.

Hilary opened the door before she reached for her key, and pulled her inside.

"Mavis, you look worn out. No. Don't say one word. We will have a meal first. I heated up lasagna while I was waiting. There's warm crusty bread and a glass of wine if you want it. I just shoved an apple pie into the oven for dessert."

It was not the thought of delicious hot food that undid Mavis. Rather, it was the warmth of Hilary's comforting voice and the normal appearance of her home, so different from the clinical place from which she had come. The tears rolled down her face without her volition and Hilary knew at once what to do. She removed the coat, placed the purse in the closet and put her arms around her friend leading her into the kitchen and settling her on one of the padded stools at the counter where she had placed a mug of hot tea as soon as she heard Mavis's car arriving. She added a box of tissues and removed herself to give the private Mavis time to recover her equilibrium. In spite of her curiosity she kept her promise and spoke casually about the day's meeting while they ate.

"Honor seems like a good candidate. I think we can accommodate her needs and since she is young she should recover well from her hip operation.

I must say I am more and more impressed with Vilma. I judged her too soon as a glamour type, likely to be overly concerned with her appearance, but I am delighted to acknowledge I was quite wrong. She has taken Jannice O'Connor under her wing. Did you see how much better Jannice looked today? Vilma may keep all of us on our toes as far as appearance is concerned."

She waited, until colour returned to Mavis's face and she had finished the plateful of lasagna and broccoli, before continuing.

"Now, if you feel stronger, tell me what has happened with Eve."

Mavis took a last sip of the glass of red wine and told her friend everything that she saw and heard at the hospital. She left to the end of her account what she had told the social worker.

"I acted on instinct with her, Hilary, and I believe I judged her correctly. We were on the same page as it were, and I think she will support my suggestion. How do you feel about it all?"

"Mavis Montgomery, I do not ever question your instincts. From the first moment you were concerned about that poor woman, Eve, and providing her with a safe place to live is part of our mandate for co-housing. We said we wanted to share living with like-minded people. Would we two, both products of caring professions, be happy without a project to improve the lives of those around us? We want harmony in our house and that will have challenges, of course."

"Hilary, I should know better than to doubt your generosity of spirit. We will work together to help Eve and Honor, and I think you have just named our future home. *Harmony House* is a perfect name. All we have to do now is find the place!"

CHAPTER 10

Snow continued to fall until the entire city of London, Ontario, was wrapped in sound-muffling, pure white. Traffic in the subdivision slowed to a crawl, schools were closed for the day, the gardens were blanketed in snow and the ever-greens began to take on the role of major land marks that were rightly theirs in winter. It seemed as if everyone took a deep breath, accepting that winter had arrived and girding themselves for the snow removal activities that would eventually give them access to the outer world again.

Mavis and Hilary chose to use this time cocooned inside, with their first log fire burning in the living room. Mavis had moved into Hilary's second bedroom for the time being. They decided to make use of the time to start the search for a future home and Hilary had a collection of local estate agents' flyers and the computer to show them where and what was on offer.

"We have our quota of six now, so we are ready to think of the next step. We need to know exactly what finances will be required from each of us for the purchase."

"I have the final papers to sign for the transfer of my house, Hilary. Yours is up for sale, Eve has the cash in her bank, Vilma is well supplied and Honor was not worried about her contribution. Jannice's place may take longer to sell but Vilma is advising her about that. I believe we are well on our way so let's take a look to see what is available."

The search was both fascinating and frustrating. Winter is not the best time to be looking for houses to buy although what was available was often discounted for a hopeful end-of-year late sale. One additional advantage of these offerings was that the advertising photographs had been taken much earlier in the year so the grounds and access roads were clearly visible. Google maps soon showed more than the agents' photos which often featured the best view and eliminated how close the neighbouring homes were placed.

They were looking for a large home, on a reasonable size of lot, not far from town and transportation links. They hoped to find a sound structure that would accommodate some renovations without difficulty. They wanted nothing too old or outdated. They required modern electric services, a good heating furnace, and plumbing in all the right locations.

Six bedrooms and six washrooms soon eliminated all the most recent building estates in London which featured mostly small multi-units and small lots. They were obliged to look further afield to the outskirts of the city, some parts of which had been absorbed into London within the last two decades.

"No one builds large homes these days," observed Hilary. "We have limited choices; either a much older stately home downtown or a newer one in a very expensive enclave."

Mavis had been leafing through their collection of Real Estate magazines looking for something unusual.

"There might be a possibility on the outskirts where the remaining farmland exists. The farms are gone now but I see one or two very nice traditional farm buildings with a bit of acreage around them still."

They discarded the oldest ones on offer despairing of yellow brick facades and large barns in the rear on rural routes. The two were on their second cups of tea when Mavis spotted a charming, large home with a traditional look, balconies and some Victorian features.

"Well it looks interesting. What do the specifications say?"

Mavis read silently for a minute absorbing the details.

"I must say, this is highly unusual in several ways. It states the home has been vacant for almost a year and there's a phrase here which is concerning."

Hilary was more and more intrigued. "Tell me!"

Mavis read aloud. "This large property was formerly owned by a developer who adapted it to suit his needs. The style may not please all clients but it is very well worth a visit from any interested parties."

"That *is* strange Mavis. What do you think it means?"

"I suspect it means we should continue looking!"

They agreed to do this and several more hours over two days were occupied in surfing the internet in a search for the perfect property. By the time they had a list of three possibilities in different parts of the city, the snow had been cleared from the main streets and the two friends were becoming impatient to check out the prospects.

"Let's take a look around. Nothing formal. No agents yet. We can combine it with a grocery shopping trip and you will be able to check in with Eve. The social worker, Sheila was it? she said Eve might be discharged today."

"Right. If we start out early we can do everything in one trip. Your car has the best road-holding reputation, Hilary, and the GPS as well. I'll pay for a fill-up. Just let me talk to the social worker before we leave."

In minutes they were on the road with a time-saving plan. Their first stop was in North London where two prospective homes were located. They found the first in a street of handsome older brick homes but Hilary dismissed both at once.

"These won't do at all. They are too close to Western University and will likely have been student residences purchased by wealthy parents for their kids' use during their university years. Not only will the interiors have been abused but the whole area will be plagued with noise complaints and piles of reject furniture on the sidewalks at the end of spring term."

"Yes, I have read something about these problems in the newspaper. It's too bad. There are a lot of downtown amenities here as well as access to events in the various colleges. Let's move on."

The second location was in a newer subdivision called Sunningdale. A mix of housing styles looked attractive. Among these were several large homes which might accommodate the number of bedrooms they needed, although there were only a few with decent space around them.

As they were driving along looking for the sale sign, Mavis suddenly realized she knew the name of the street.

"Stop, Hilary! This is where Vilma lives. We couldn't choose a house in this area without making Vilma highly uncomfortable."

Hilary turned the car around at once and drove back to Richmond Street. Mavis consulted their 'Top Choices' list and suggested trying Wortley Village.

"It's an award winning area. Not large. Central to downtown and has plenty in the way of restaurants, coffee shops and even a library branch and a grocery store."

"That sounds more promising!"

The first thing Hilary saw as she drove into Wortley Village was the open ground around a very stately building.

"Look! A spot to walk a dog! This is the original Normal School for training teachers but that was well before my time. It has changed hands recently. I am pleased they retained the green space here."

"Not only that, one of London's oldest parks is just around the corner near a branch of the River Thames."

"You're right. I'll park here at the grocery store and we can walk about."

Once they traversed the length of Wortley Village admiring the variety of amenities, they found the street where the house for sale stood. It was very large, Victorian in design with projecting wings and superstructure and had a sign indicating it belonged to the nearby parish church.

They looked at it in silence for a few minutes without commenting.

"It's dark looking with these huge old trees."

"The exterior stone work needs cleaning."

"Do you think it has been used as a hostel of some kind?"

"Possibly. It could have many small rooms inside."

"The windows are smaller than I like."

"Yes."

"Would they ring the bell in that church tower every Sunday?"

"Nice area though."

"Absolutely!"

On the walk back to the car, Mavis looked at her watch and knew they needed to head for the hospital quite soon. Sheila had confirmed Eve was to be discharged and she requested a minute to update Mavis before they left for home with Eve.

They decided to do a quick run around the grocery store first, to collect the basics as the car was already in the parking lot.

It was only a five minute journey to the hospital. Mavis spent the time going over in her head all the arrangements she had made for Eve's arrival at Camden Corners. The second bedroom had two single beds and she was more than willing to share with Eve.

"She has been through a dreadful experience. I can watch over her at night and make sure she does not overexert herself. She is still recuperating."

"That's so good of you, Mavis. It means you have decided to leave Emery Street and move in with me. What shall we tell the others at the next meeting?"

"I don't see the necessity to tell them anything yet. Hopefully Eve can attend the meeting. It will be obvious she has not been well. Nothing else is required for now. I imagine she will fill in some details for them when she feels she knows us better."

"We don't have any information to give the others about the house search so far."

"No. Not so far. If the weather holds we can start again soon."

~

Eve Dobrinski had been moved out of Emergency into a short-term ward in the main hospital. Sheila was waiting for them there. When the doctor signed the discharge papers, Eve could leave, but Sheila had some further information for Mavis.

They moved to a lounge at the end of the corridor for privacy. Sheila began by saying she had passed on Mavis's plan to her superiors and it was approved.

"Of course, the matter is now in police hands. There will be an enquiry as to the abuse but my impression is that Eve will not press charges against her husband."

Mavis grimaced at this news. The statistics demonstrated how often this was the case with battered wives. Because she knew well the harrowing court procedures of such cases she was not surprised to hear Eve's decision.

"I imagine she just wants to be done with the whole nasty business and start again."

"Unfortunately, there is a problem about that. The hospital staff on this floor informed me Howard Dobrinski attempted to pay a visit to his wife. He was irate about her disappearance and the fact he was contacted about their health insurance number before he even knew where his wife was.

The doctor in charge was determined to keep the angry man away from Eve as he felt she was fragile in health. This did not help matters as you can guess. Dobrinski stormed back to Reception and found out about the 'cousin' who enquired about her. Unfortunately, your address was given to him shortly before he was escorted out of the building."

Mavis swore under her breath. She had written Hilary's address on the next-of-kin form. The situation was now much more complicated but she knew what the next step must be. A police order to ban Howard Dobrinski from approaching his wife must be put in place as soon as possible and that meant Eve was required to swear out a statement.

"Thank you for putting me in the picture, Sheila. I will take care of this as soon as Eve is fit.

You can assure your supervisors that Eve will be in good hands with us. Hilary's home has a security system and we will immediately block any calls from the husband."

Wishing them good luck, Sheila went off on her way and Mavis returned to the ward to find Eve dressed and ready to go. She smiled when her slouch hat appeared from Mavis's purse.

"Let's go home now," Hilary said.

Mavis said nothing about the new problems. She would let Eve settle in and rest before breaking the bad news to Hilary.

CHAPTER 11

Two weeks passed before the topic of a house purchase was raised again.

In the intervening time, Eve Barton blossomed in a way Hilary could not believe. It was as if the weight of the world had been removed from her slim shoulders.

Hilary searched her dresser drawers and unearthed a selection of silk scarves small enough to be folded into headbands to conceal the scars on Eve's head which were more obvious now, since the doctors had shaved the area. Tied to one side, these scarves were colourful and attractive additions to the clothing both Mavis and Hilary contributed to Eve's new wardrobe. It was amazing what a difference a little colour in a blouse or sweater made to the younger woman's attitude. She grew stronger by the day and although she refused to enter her old house to retrieve her belongings, she agreed to visit the police station with Mavis to swear out a warrant against her husband.

Despite her misgivings, Howard Dobrinski had not appeared on their doorstep for which Hilary was most grateful. She had employed a company to come to the house and install an outdoor camera. It came with a company sign, large enough to serve as a deterrent to any passerby with criminal ideas.

"He may be afraid to come storming in here with three women against him. These abusers are cowards at heart."

Mavis said nothing to this. She was aware of cases where abusers never ceased their reign of terror until they had killed the partner who they professed to love. She remained on high alert, particularly during the night and walked around the property every morning looking for large footprints in the snow, camera in hand, to provide evidence she could present to the police. She also placed a baseball bat in a corner of the hall closet, just in case.

Eve was strong enough to join the group for the next

meeting. It was not surprising to Hilary when curious glances were cast in Eve's direction. She was almost unrecognizable from the cowed and pale woman who had appeared briefly at previous meetings. She volunteered to take on the role of kitchen supervisor and handed around plates of mini muffins which she had made, filling tea cups when needed. She did not speak much but her comfort level was rising with every brief encounter. These were to be her future companions and she was beyond happy at the prospect of her new life to come.

The meeting topic was 'Weeding Possessions and House Contents'. Mavis began with the information that her former home was now sold to a delightful couple with a child.

"The family are thrilled with the heritage home and have purchased most of the furnishings. There are only a few items I wish to keep for my future shared home and those, with most of my clothes, have been moved into a storage unit. Needless to say, I am very happy there will be a little girl growing up in the attic bedroom so carefully finished by my late husband.

I say all this to encourage others to move ahead with the task of planning what they will need and what needs to be recycled or shared or otherwise disposed of."

Vilma responded with the information that she would be buying new furnishings when she had an idea of the size of the room she would eventually occupy.

"But," she continued, "I am happy to help others with resources. Jannice and I are compiling a list of local places where unwanted goods can go and we have already started the process of clearing out her very old house packed with belongings."

Hilary offered her thanks to Vilma with a warm smile. "Storage facilities are an option for the short term as Mavis suggested, but others here might want the chance to see what is being discarded."

She was thinking of Eve who had expressed no interest in retrieving anything from her prior unhappy home.

Honor Pace spoke up for the first time. "I won't need any furniture but I am interested in the recycling idea. I will investigate online resources and coordinate with Vilma and Jannice." Here she exchanged an enquiring look with Vilma, who was pleased to nod her approval. "I know of charities that assist with providing supplies for Syrian refugees, for example, but I am sure I can come up with some other ideas. For instance, I know a company that will film and store old photos and other items and give you a record so you don't forget what and where your things are."

"That is so helpful, Honor. I must say, ladies, I love the way we are blending together into a cohesive group. It bodes well for our future."

Mavis saw Hilary's smile pass around the room as everyone showed their agreement. She felt now was a good point at which to indicate the latest on the house search.

"Hilary and I have begun the process of searching for our future home. Don't get too excited! There's a long way to go on this and we have time. We have looked around at some likely prospects but no decisions as yet. We have not contacted any agents and are keeping in mind your requirements.

Oh, Honor, do you have anything to add to that list?"

"I believe I mentioned my preference for a ground level room but I must have WiFi access in order to run my business. I own a computer and printer of course, and I already have a storage unit for business records and supplies."

"Good. This is the kind of detail we can work with. Keep thinking ahead, everyone, and do relish the last Christmas in your present accommodations. Some of you will have family festivities to attend.

We'll meet again after the holidays in a new year which should be an exciting one for all of us."

An hour of further discussion, coffee and tea drinking, and exchange of personal information ensued. Hilary noted these sessions were becoming longer as the connections between them grew stronger.

She closed the front door behind Honor, after watching her progress down the steps. Honor declared she was much more mobile now and could manage on her own but Hilary was taking no chances. She thought she caught a brief glimpse of a hooded figure vanishing between two houses across the road but quickly turned her attention back to Honor until she safely drove away in a cab.

"Well, then Eve. How did you feel about the meeting?"

Eve looked up from piling the dishes beside the dishwasher and replied that she could not wait to live together with these wonderful, supportive women. "I am so grateful for your help, Hilary, and Mavis too, of course. I feel like I have a chance to my start my life over again but, if you don't mind, I will go upstairs for a nap once these dishes are loaded."

Mavis shooed Eve away at once and when she

had gone she suggested Eve would be a candidate for some of Hilary's unwanted furniture.

"You are right! I'll tackle that when she is back to her full strength and can make decisions."

Their talk resumed with the topic of Christmas decorations. Mavis knew how devoted her friend was to the Christmas season's displays of colourful lights and special ornaments. She had seen for herself the large section of the basement devoted to the storage of such seasonal treasures and she did not relish the job of informing Hilary most of the accumulation would have to go in the new year. Let her enjoy it for the last time, she thought, with a quiet chuckle. She would refuse to be a part of that decision process.

She intended to offer the very traditional Christmas items she and Peter had gathered over the years to the new family, as they were particularly suited to the style and age of the Ontario Cottage. If she ever felt nostalgia for such a look again she would simply make a visit to Eldon House and bask in the flavour of the restored 1834 historic home in London where generations of the Harris family once lived in Victorian splendour.

When Hilary woke suddenly in the middle of the

night she remembered the glimpse of the dark figure she had seen across the road earlier in the day, then promptly forgotten. She decided to accompany Mavis on her daily patrol in the morning and keep an eye out for other strangers in the future.

~

Snow continued over Christmas and New Year's celebrations. Eve decided to cook a turkey and Mavis added roast potatoes, stuffing and vegetables to the feast. Hilary insisted on mashed turnip which was a favourite of her mother's and she promised a surprise dessert, not made of turnip, she insisted, to laughter from the others.

With three women in the house, it was a mini preview of how it would be by next Christmas when they were, hopefully, installed in their new forever home. A certain amount of juggling was required in the kitchen area and also in the main bathroom. Eve preferred to bathe or shower in the evenings, while Mavis and Hilary had a routine in the mornings to accommodate earlier risers. Hilary believed this experience would allow the two friends to eventually share one washroom if that turned out to be necessary. It was one of the many adjustments Hilary was noting. Six women in one house was not a project to be taken on without a considerable amount of pre-planning and that was her forte.

For now, it was delightful to share the season with Mavis and Eve. It was entirely different from her lonely time a year before. The sound of happy voices in other parts of the house while she worked on plans, made her heart soar.

On the second day of the new year, they mounted an expedition to see prospective houses. Several had dropped out of the list for the winter months but there were a few possibilities and the streets were quiet with many workers taking a longer break over Christmas and New Year.

Eve was very excited to be included and she sat in the rear seat with the sheaf of pamphlets and flyers beside her for reference. This time they began on the fringes of London. There was a large subdivision in Lambeth, quite hidden from the main street, which had the spacious homes and half-acre plots they were seeking. Lambeth had a number of facilities and access to downtown via Wharncliffe Road was fast.

Mavis observed several newer housing estates in the area and although these homes were not what they were looking for, they would mean more business and amenities would arrive in time.

They drove around the silent subdivision

watching for sale signs but nothing was available. Hilary estimated the homes here would be nearer the two million dollar mark and many of the residents were likely wintering in Florida, Mexico, or other sunny climes.

"A trifle rich for our blood, ladies!" she exclaimed. She was beginning to wonder if they could manage to wait until the spring brought more houses for sale. The issue of establishing costs and setting up financial arrangements might not wait that long and interim housing would be an expense they could ill afford.

Another hour passed in fruitless searching, until Mavis remembered the information about the unusual house they had not actually seen in their previous searches.

"It was the one with the odd description. Should we look there just for fun? It's our last try of the day and we should be heading home soon. Mavis had her eye on the car's gas gauge. She had a horror of running out of gas in winter and being stranded in the cold on some side street far from help.

Hilary related the details and Eve soon found the original newspaper clipping.

Vacant for a year or more.

Owned by a developer.

Unusual property.

Quiet location.

When Eve read out the price, Hilary and Mavis looked across at each other with the same thought. Something must be wrong with the place. The price was nearer 750,000 dollars, twice the average for a detached house in London, Ontario, but less than such a property was worth, judging from the photograph of the exterior.

Employing the GPS, Hilary found the property at Westdel Bourne which was away from the main roads but not that far from Byron and shopping, doctors and other necessities.

They pulled up at the end of a long driveway and looked toward the house which was covered in a layer of snow, hiding many of its features.

There was silence in the car for several minutes then the comments began.

It looks big enough to accommodate six.

The style is more Niagara-On-The-Lake than stuffy old London.

I love that small turret bit on one side.

There's a wrap-around porch. Wonderful for the summer!

That's a big front lawn. We would need a gardener.

The windows are lovely.

The architectural details I can see are charming.

Where's the garage?

What's beyond those trees?

It would be a nightmare if the roof had to be replaced.

The style is Victorian meets the Deep South but it does not look that old at all.

I like it.

I do too.

Eve was mostly listening. She felt as if her opinion should not hold sway in this decision but she was excited to think a beautiful home like this might even be considered. It was a dream come true.

"What's your thought, Eve?"

"I am entranced! That's not very logical, of course. More of an emotional reaction."

"We do have to have our practical heads on."

Hilary brought them back to reality again. "We can't judge only by the exterior, although I admit that is quite remarkable. There's the troubling matter of the developer and the description 'unusual' which might cover a number of construction sins."

Mavis glanced down at her watch and up at the lowering clouds which would likely hold more snow.

"If I may summarize, we need to contact the realtor and arrange a viewing. I think we are all in agreement that this one demands more attention."

With that, Hilary turned the car around and they made their way back to Camden Corners. Each of the car's passengers was immersed in thought. Seeing a possible candidate for their future home made the whole scheme of shared housing much more of a reality.

Eve was excited.

Mavis was wondering how they would allocate the desirable tower room.

Hilary was thinking she must contact her realtor about the progress of her own house sale and also find out who represented the 'Niagara' house. There was no point in getting too enthusiastic about it before they saw the interior realities. It was essential to keep in mind their list of requirements. There were six individuals to be satisfied. She did retain a touch of comfort from the fact that three of the six had been pleased, about the exterior at least. Of course, the remaining three might not be so easy to please.

Not one of the women noticed the trodden snow at the side of their current home in the rush to get inside and warm up.

CHAPTER 12

Hilary Dempster had been well schooled in safety measures by her husband who was very conscious of the value of property and the need for good maintenance. He had left her a schedule for changing furnace filters and having regular inspections of heating and cooling systems. Since Eve had joined them, Hilary was even more particular about being the last person to lock up before going to bed. She would walk around, checking windows, adjusting the heating for the night and listening for dripping taps. She was also responsible for the garbage collection schedule and although Mavis insisted on taking the bags and recycling boxes to the curb, Hilary would do a last look around the garage to see that nothing had been left behind.

It was as she was standing by the switch to close the garage doors that she suddenly saw footprints that were obvious not those of Mavis who had just finished placing the recycling by the street side of the driveway and gone up to bed.

Hilary had a strange feeling of discomfort and remembered the dark figure she had glimpsed. She already had winter boots on her feet to avoid the wet floor of the garage. She quickly grabbed a spare coat hanging on a peg and walked out carrying a torch from a shelf in the garage.

In only a few moments she could see the footprints that did not belong there. Treading carefully, so as not to obliterate the evidence, she followed along the side of the house to the tall wooden gate leading to the back yard. Someone had pushed open the gate in the fence, using a considerable amount of force to overcome the resistance of the snow piled up behind it. The footsteps continued for a few more steps then stopped for some time as the impressions were deeper in one spot. She began to imagine what the intruder could see from that spot and realized he would have a good view of the living room including all of the people sitting there to watch television.

Of course, it must have been Howard Dobrinski. A red rage flooded her mind obliterating any fear she might have of encountering the man on his nasty spying missions. He had tracked down Eve and now he was watching the house and its occupants. Immediately after the rage filled her, she was incensed by the realization the expensive security camera had not given her any warning of this. She left the footprints in place and continued over to the other side of the house where a walkway gave access to the side door of the garage. She would close the garage and enter the house without making any comments. She would not alarm Eve or Mavis at this time of night.

Better they should sleep in peace for now.

As for herself, she went swiftly to her office, closed the door and dialed the number of the security firm. They must have a film record of the surroundings of the house which could be used as evidence when she went to the police to inform them Howard Dobrinski had broken the bonds of his warrant to stay away from his wife. She intended to get action on this matter after which she would castigate the manager of the company about the serious deficiency in the protection promised to his customers.

Early the next morning, Hilary informed Mavis not to bother doing her usual patrol with the camera. It had snowed heavily during the night so Mavis was glad of the warning although she thought her friend looked tired and anxious as she said it.

After breakfast, during which the topic of discussion was the 'Niagara House' as they called it, Hilary said she had some errands to do and she drove off without any further explanation.

Mavis decided it would be a good time to ask Eve if there were any items of Hilary's furniture she might want for her bedroom in the shared house. She needed to have an idea of Eve's requirements in case Hilary's sale came up quickly and things began to move rapidly. Eve was reluctant to claim anything for herself but decided the single bed she was sleeping in suited her well and she would be glad of any other items not needed by her hostess.

"The furniture in this lovely house is mostly teak wood so all the pieces fit together so well. I would be pleased with anything, but I really need very little. I think your kitchen supplies could be moved straight into the new home if that suits everyone. The toaster and microwave and the coffee maker are all new appliances."

"Not a bad idea. I suppose all of us would like to have some facility to make a hot drink in our rooms."

Mavis made a mental note to talk to Hilary about whether electric appliances in rooms required special safety permissions. This business of sharing a home was not going to be a simple process.

Hilary's expedition to the Police Headquarters downtown on Dundas Street did not go as well as she had expected. A sergeant behind the desk recognized her as his former teacher and ushered her into a small office, accompanied by a running commentary of fond memories of his days at school.

"Derek!" she interrupted, after five minutes of this. "I don't have time for reminiscences today. I am here on a serious matter. I have reason to believe a member of my household is being stalked by her husband, a man who has abused her and who is under warrant to stay away from his wife."

Sergeant Derek Price immediately blinked hard and resumed his normal mode of efficient professionalism.

"Oh, I see! When did you come to this conclusion?" He began to make notes.

"Yesterday, I found a set of large footprints around my residence after previously noticing a stranger in the neighbourhood."

"You say there is a formal complaint against this man? What is his name and address?"

"Look, Sergeant Price, you can find all this out

easily. What I am most concerned about is our safety. There are three women living in my home and I have just discovered the safety camera I had installed shows only a dark, hooded figure. I am afraid by the time we can identify this intruder on my property, it may be too late."

She stopped and tried to breathe normally. She had not intended to let her concerns come out in such a dramatic fashion but once said aloud, she realized she *was* really afraid and it must have been obvious to her listener.

Derek Price hid his surprise. He had never seen his highly-respected teacher exhibit such uncertainty and he immediately decided to help, even if it was not strictly standard procedure.

"Right then, Mrs. Dempster, leave it with me. Give me your address and contact information and I will make sure a patrol car checks your location today. We will talk to neighbours and see if there are any sightings of this man. Don't be worried. We'll soon apprehend him and the courts will deal with him."

He rose to escort her out and managed to stop himself from patting her arm. It would feel good to do something to help this fine woman who had had such a positive influence on the lives of several people he could name.

Hilary pulled up her coat collar against the blowing snow and decided not to alarm her companions until it was absolutely necessary. Eve was still in a fragile state and the worry would be detrimental to her recovery. For now, she would leave everything in the hands of the police.

With the decision made, she drove carefully through town and headed back home. The next thing on her mind was her Real Estate agent. She needed to know if there was any activity related to her house sale. There was now a new urgency about moving out of Camden Corners to a location unknown to one Howard Dobrinski. The topic of the next group meeting must be a better focus on the amount of money required for the proposed joint house purchase.

Mavis presumed Hilary was seeing her realtor. She was still thinking about the 'Niagara House' and wondering if the cost was prohibitive. There was only one way to find out. She retrieved the news-paper clipping and gave the listed agent a call. At the very least she would get more information and save Hilary the trouble of removing the house from their list of possibilities.

To her surprise, the agent, a man with a young and pleasant voice, answered at the second ring.

"Evan Mahavolich here. How may I help you?"

"Ah, I am enquiring about a property you have listed on Belleview Crescent."

There was a slight pause during which Mavis could hear the clacking of computer keys.

"Yes, a very interesting property. If you wish to view it, I need a day or two of warning so I can get the driveway and the porch cleared of snow."

"At the moment, I, *we,* are seeking further information regarding price, availability et cetera."

"I see. Well, it has been vacant for some time and I believe I can get a reduction in price from the owner if that is an incentive for you?"

There was another pause. She could almost hear his brain clicking over.

"The owner suggests a guide price of $750,000 but it is a large home with many attractive features and well worth a look."

The price was as ridiculously low as Mavis had thought. For such a large property it indicated something was far wrong. It might still be a serious contender as a shared home. Everything would depend on the condition of both the exterior and interior.

"Mr. Mahavolich…"

"Please call me Evan."

"Evan, it's winter. It's cold outside, I need to know more about the condition of the house but I will say on behalf of others who would be involved, that there is a certain amount of interest here already."

"Mrs. Dempster, I will be honest with you. This lovely property in an excellent setting, as you would have seen, needs an unusual purchaser."

Here it comes! The word 'unusual' again. He can identify who the caller is from the phone number. I won't correct him. He knows enough already.

"The outer appearance is not similar to the interior. The home is only a few years old and in good condition but the developer made the mistake of trying to do two different things to please his wife, I believe. You see, the traditional style of the house is not carried through inside the property.

Some clients have stated that there is a stark contrast between them."

Mavis tried to work her way through this description and come out with a conclusion. Evan was not being straight with her, despite his promise.

"Do you mean the inside is modern?"

"Exactly!"

"How modern? Ultra modern? She was imagining black walls and murals and strange metal accents that would jar with the charming features of the exterior.

"Nothing too extreme for you, I am sure. I can

send you some photographs and you can judge for yourself. Remember, of course, that many interior items, like décor, are inexpensive to alter."

Another red flag!

"Please do that Evan. I will call again if we want to arrange a viewing. Thank you."

Well, this explains the length of time without a purchase, the use of the word 'unusual' and the remarkably low price. I will inform Hilary when she gets home, and hope the photos are not too shocking.

CHAPTER 13

Honor Pace was enthused by her reception at Camden Corners. Everyone seemed welcoming and there was no liability in her late introduction to the shared-home project. No one had questioned her about finances which gave her sufficient time to gather her resources. A new home had not yet been purchased and from what she could determine from the meeting, most of the participants had some kind of preparation to complete before the move. This all fit into her plan to get physically stronger and be able to pursue her business from a new location as long as it was not too far out of London.

When a deposit of some kind to retain the property was requested, she would be ready.

In the meantime she would enjoy these women and learn more about them. After all, she was relinquishing a solitary, confined existence in favour of a possible lifetime with five females who would all have their quirks and preferences. Mavis and Hilary seemed nice on the surface but until she was confident about the actual details of the legal agreement and the nature of the investment particulars, she would not be fully committed to the venture. She dared not risk her savings on some get-rich-quick scheme.

Perhaps this is a way I can help out, she thought. I have clients who are financial wizards and I maintain computer programs for a company of lawyers. When I see the details, I can ask these experts to vet the viability of the plan.

She glanced around her small apartment. Whatever was on offer at the shared home would be an improvement on her present accommodations. She would leave behind anything that did not fit her new space. It was time to alert the building manager he would have another space to rent within the next six months.

~

Jannice O'Connor was glad she had overcome her

fear of allowing Vilma into her home. The results were heartening in so many ways.

"Look, girl!" Vilma had declared as soon as she entered the dingy front door, "I may be a fancy dresser with a perfect house at my disposal but that doesn't mean I started out in life with these advantages.

I was born in Prince Edward County, Ontario, on a farm with four older brothers and parents who worked like slaves every hour of the day and some of the night as well. My brothers made sure I was as strong as they were but at the same time they protected me from other farm boys. They had ambitions not only for their own futures but also for mine. A life of drudgery in the countryside was not for them.

We all struggled at school. Only by dint of helping each other did we pass the exams and move on to higher education. We were like a team. When guys approached me for dates in high school, they had to go through my brothers first. The result was that I was able to concentrate on school and finally move on to a kind of charm school where I got an agent and good work as a model. I had a lot of success because I knew about hard work and my brothers had never allowed me to get a 'swelled head'. They treated me like another one of the team and made no allowances for my looks.

At first one of the boys would accompany me to photoshoots but when I was asked to travel to the United States and beyond, I was finally on my own.

It was on one of those swimwear photoshoots on an island in the Caribbean when I was spotted by a handsome younger son of a rich family who spent most of the winters in their vacation home in the sun. I fell for him like the proverbial ton of bricks. He was my first love. He introduced me to a lifestyle I had only seen in movies. I was in way over my head but the values my brothers had instilled in me kept me from becoming immersed in the extravagances of the rich and vacuous.

Vaughan persuaded his father we should marry soon and it all happened very fast. I was a trophy wife, shown around at parties. I suppose I was something new in their circles; unspoiled and feisty about my beliefs.

We returned to New York and more parties, more fancy restaurants and more spending. Eventually, and I am ashamed it took as long as it did take, I rebelled for the last time. My husband made the fatal mistake of chasing after a very pretty waitress in a restaurant we used for business acquaintances in his family's banking empire. I quickly found out he was staying overnight with her in a hotel.

My first instinct was to cry my heart out, but I recovered fast and called my oldest brother in Toronto. He flew down and whisked me out of there. I made him promise not to lay a finger on Vaughan or I would stay married to him.

As we waited in the airport to fly back to Canada, I reviewed my disaster of a relationship and vowed never to get involved with a young, empty-headed, juvenile again."

Jannice was listening to this vivid account open-mouthed and amazed. It was like a movie. She could see all the scenes rolling by in her head as Vilma spoke. The movie stopped abruptly as Vilma broke out into wild laughter.

"I swear, Jannice, I was such an idiot! I got the divorce and started over in Toronto. What I did next proved my lunacy for all time. I met an older man at the office where I worked as receptionist. He insisted on taking me for dinner each time he came to town. He was a perfect gentleman who treated me with respect. I had no idea he had made a deal with my bosses that I was to be available as a dinner partner whenever he was in Toronto. When he offered to buy me a swanky apartment in a highrise hotel, I slapped his face and fled, only to discover the next day that I had been fired for 'insubordination'.

I may have been stupid, but I had acquired a few ideas along the way including one about my rights as an employee. I found a firm of lawyers on the internet. One of those firms who insist there are no fees up front until they win your case. The lawyers were delighted to sue such a big company. Their investigator found two more girls who had been dismissed for similar trumped-up reasons, and the company soon settled with me rather than have their name dragged through the courts.

I lived quietly on that settlement for several years until I met my Nolan. On our first date he told me about his divorce. I told him about my chequered past which he refused to believe, preferring to think my style and manner were more natural than acquired through experience. At last I had the genuine article in him. We married and I helped him in his showroom where he sold high-end motor cars from Italy. We had many wonderful holidays together in Europe and I loved him dearly until the day he died."

"That is an amazing story! What a pity his children did not admire you as they should have done."

"Well, Jannice, it's hard to get perfection. I was

very happy with Nolan and I believe he felt the same about me. I count my blessings every day."

"So, you want me to know you are no stranger to hard work and I shouldn't expect you to go off and marry again?"

Vilma laughed that infectious laugh.

"You could put it like that, I suppose. In the meantime, let's get the oldest junk in here ready for the remover and we will see what else needs doing before we stage this place for its new owners. I predict a decorator with lots of paint will be required."

Vilma was as good as her word. She rolled up her sleeves and they began to select and eject most of the furniture left over from past generations. For Jannice O'Connor it was as if a breath of fresh air had entered her life and this lovely woman had appeared like an angel exactly when most needed.

～

Hilary's appointment with her realtor produced two offers to buy her house.

"I will need you to vacate the premises for a few hours so I can show the clients around. I think the representative of Fanshawe College is the best bet, but I have already informed him there is a competitive bidder also interested in purchasing. I wouldn't do too much in the way of changing the furnishings or anything else, since the chances are it will be knocked down and replaced fairly soon.

Just tidy up a bit. You know the score."

Hilary could have been offended at this casual dismissal of her family home, but she had mentally moved on already and there was no point in needless emotion. A quick sale was desirable for several reasons as long as the price was appropriate.

She made a note of the date and time of the showings and drove home to break the news to Mavis and Eve.

No sooner had she taken off her coat and headed to the kitchen than Mavis appeared from the office where she had been printing the photos Evan had sent.

"Glad you are home, Hilary! Wait till you see this. Evan has sent them on and he says he had the driveway and porch cleared already so we can go for a look as soon as we like."

"Who is Evan? What photos? What's been going on here?"

"Oh, sit down and I'll explain everything. Eve, will you put on the kettle for us? I'll bring you both up to speed."

She proceeded to tell Hilary all she had done

with regard to the Niagara House. The colour photos were soon spread out on the island counter top.

"I'm afraid I can't figure these out at all. The interior looks very strange to me."

"I agree, Eve. What makes you think this is a good candidate, Mavis? It looks like a madman has gone wild with paint in this place."

"Try to ignore the décor, ladies. The good news is that the house is underpriced at $750,000 and Evan says an even better deal can be made with the owner. Before you protest, Hilary, there are six bedrooms and more space in the full basement which has a walkout at the rear. The house has five full bathrooms already and the electrical system is state of the art. There's an updated furnace, forced air heating and cooling, a spacious separate garage building and very pretty gardens at the rear. It's almost perfect for our needs and a mere five minute drive to access roads into Byron Village. *And* it's on a crescent with four other substantial houses so we would not be alone if help were needed."

Mavis paused for breath. Hilary and Eve glanced at each other and saw similar expressions of surprise.

"Well, now, you seem to be convinced this is our house, Mavis dear!"

"I may have laid it on rather thick, Hilary, but I have a good feeling about this one. It sounds like exactly what we need. What do you think about seeing it soon? Evan is ready to take us around."

Hilary made a quick calculation. If she could get these two women to help with the cleanup for her own two viewings, they could go out to see the Niagara House on the same day, leaving Camden Court to her realtor. She felt quite keen to meet this Evan who had swayed the usually-practical Mavis so quickly.

In her own mind she reserved judgement. She expected the weird interior décor might be so outrageous that it overwhelmed all other factors.

"The timing could work out very well, Mavis. Once I tell you both *my* house news you will see what I mean."

She would say nothing about the police visit until young Sergeant Price had forwarded his report.

No need to worry Eve or Mavis unduly.

At least not yet.

CHAPTER 14

It was a very busy three days. Despite everything her realtor had said about not doing too much, Hilary wanted her house scoured and any extraneous items removed to the basement so the space seemed even larger than it was. She put cinnamon rolls to bake slowly in the oven, sprayed air freshener in the bathrooms and took a last walk around to make sure everything was immaculate. As far as she was concerned, a suggestion her house might be purchased by Fanshawe College was just that... a suggestion. A buyer might well be a family seeking a good solid house and if that occurred she was now confident they would see an appealing possibility in 46, Camden Corners.

She hustled Mavis and Eve along and closed the

front door behind them, placing the key safely in the realtor's lock box. She was pleased the house would not be left empty while its occupants were viewing the Niagara house and she promised herself she would tell both women of her efforts to apprehend Howard Dobrinski on their return home.

The atmosphere in the car was part anticipation and part fear of disappointment. The snow had settled down and roads and sidewalks were cleared. The sun shone brightly again in a clear blue sky but the air was frigid.

Evan was standing on the swept front porch with a beaming smile on his face. Introductions were made amid some confusion as Mavis had to explain her phone call, but soon they were entering the front hall together and removing their boots.

The trio stood there absorbing the effect of a spacious entrance with a carpeted side staircase rising up to a second level balcony off which were a number of doors.

Evan was talking about 'a convenient powder room and generous coat closet' but none of the three could hear him. They were astonished at the attempt to create an ultra-modern residence inside a traditional exterior. A central lantern light high above at roof level, flooded the entry with bright sunshine which served to illuminate the vibrant colour of the carpeting (was it really that vivid a purple?), while the walls positively zinged with a sharp lemon shade that brought saliva to the mouth.

Their heads turned to the rooms on left and right hoping for relief from the eye-watering effect, only to see a blue drawing room suite so dark in tone as to appear black against a white carpet. On the right was a dining room with an ornate table and high-backed chairs set on a floral nightmare of a rug and with dark panelled walls belonging to another era entirely. To make matters worse, (was it possible?) the walls appeared to be the repository of someone's art collection. This varied from copies of Picasso's Blue Period to stark landscapes reminiscent of some of the Group of Seven.

Open mouths and in-taken breaths revealed the horror the women were experiencing. Evan seemed impervious to this reaction. He continued to extoll the virtues of the rooms without a pause until Hilary could stand it no longer and interrupted with a loud exclamation.

"Just a minute, young man! Were these people mad? This place is a nightmare. Was a decorator employed at all? What is this all about? Is the whole house like this?"

Evan gulped, chose to respond to the last impassioned question and turned to face his hoped-for future clients with rather less of a confident smile than previously.

"Oh, I believe you will be much happier with the bedrooms. Why don't we go upstairs right away, ladies. I can show you the marvellous kitchen and rear patio later."

They trooped upstairs in despair. The bedrooms would need to be exemplary to counteract the horrible effect of the first floor.

Hilary was appalled.

Eve was intrigued. She felt there was a story here.

Mavis was not too surprised. Evan's clues on the phone had given her prior warning. She still retained some small kernel of hope, nevertheless.

"There are four ensuite bedrooms within this section."

"I thought there were six bedrooms?"

Oh, this one is going to be a real buzzkill!

He composed his face and continued. "To your left through that door is the entrance to an additional substantial bedroom suite in the upper tower room. Shall we see that now, ladies?"

Mavis nodded enthusiastically. If there was anything in this place that might convince Hilary to stay longer, it would be the tower room. She crossed her fingers and hoped.

Evan turned around and walked to the door

separating the two bedroom sections. He opened the door with a theatrical flourish and invited the women to enter first.

Hilary took the lead with Mavis following behind Eve.

The tower room with three long windows and wide sills, could not have been more different from the kaleidoscope downstairs. The four-poster bed was draped in silk panels of a delicate blush hue. The furniture was set against the curved outer wall where all the pieces fit perfectly, and all were of a light beech wood. There were blinds and drapes on the windows of a similar blush pink to the bed hangings and the carpeting was wall-to-wall cream broadloom matching the delicate shade of the wall paint. Four crystal wall lights gleamed between and beside the windows and a set of matching lamps sat on two bedside tables. The bed coverings were so sumptuous they invited the viewers to touch, then lie down and rest, in total comfort in this magical setting.

Evan stood back and watched the magic take over.

"It's like a childhood dream," whispered Eve, with unconcealed longing in her voice.

Mavis was checking out the walls near the bed

for two more doors. *There must be an ensuite wash-room and a walk-in closet to make this perfect.*

"Well, that's more like it," said Hilary, grudgingly. "But it's a child's room, obviously! Not exactly suit-able for our needs."

Evan merely inclined his head. He was aware of the effect even if she was denying it. Now he had to consolidate the sale before the magic dissipated.

"Shall we take a quick look at the other bedrooms then I'll show you the second staircase leading to the modern kitchen with a spectacular view."

There was no way he was going to subject these women to the entrance hall again. A well-planned, functional kitchen was always a major selling point in his experience.

The four bedrooms seemed prosaic after the tower room's extravaganza but each was similar in size, without furniture, had an ensuite washroom, a pair of useful closets and either one or two windows.

The wall colours were more neutral but as Hilary had promised all of the women could choose their own colours, this was not a matter of concern.

The second staircase was concealed behind a double door at the opposite end of the balcony from the tower room. Evan took the lead down one flight to the kitchen. This was a show-stopper and he stood back without saying a word. The women walked around the generous space where the appliances all looked new and boasted a matched set of attractive pale green fronts. The huge island was pale grey as were the floor tiles, and the cupboards, of which there were plenty, were a slightly darker shade of grey with details picked out in darker green. The kitchen was open to a breakfast nook in front of a bay window but it was the view from the window and the sliding door exit to the deck that drew all eyes.

The garden was heaped in mounds of snow punctuated by large fir trees. There was the hint of paths winding through the beds toward a bank of trees marking the boundary of the property.

"I can assure you, ladies, this is a lovely garden. The lady of the house was most particular about the garden which she had marked out very early in the building process. In spring there will be an amazing display of colourful flowers from the hundreds of bulbs she had planted."

"So, there was a gardener working here?"

"That is correct, Mrs. Dempster."

"What's the story here, Evan? It's clear there was a great deal of money and work put into this property and now it is for sale. It cannot be very old.

There must be a reason for the sale so soon after the house was finished."

He was prepared for this question. He invited the women to sit on the comfortable sofas arranged in front of a beautiful gas fire, which he clicked on with the touch of a remote. When all were seated he began the tale. He stood by the side of the fireplace leaning on the marble mantel.

Quite the showman, our Evan, thought Hilary.

"As I mentioned before, a developer built this property for his wife. He chose the exterior stylings according to his own taste but his wife, a very forceful lady, was not pleased with any part of it when she returned to London with her daughter after spending the winter in the Bahamas. The developer insisted he could not afford to rebuild as he had invested a great deal of his available money in buying the land and having the plan designed especially to his requirements.

A huge disagreement ensued. His wife was furious. She employed a designer to reproduce the tropical setting she had enjoyed while in the Bahamas. You have seen the results. The potted banana trees have been removed.

Fortunately, she left the kitchen untouched but she made a princess palace out of the tower room for her daughter to spite her husband who had intended it as a master bedroom for the couple.

To cut a long story short, the dispute ended in divorce. Neither the wife nor the husband spent one night in this house. The daughter, who adored the tower bedroom, was here only briefly.

It was a sad and expensive venture for the developer hence the reduced cost of the house. You can see it is too large for the average family. None of my viewings has produced a reasonable offer and the developer is very keen to sell."

The unspoken comment was that the man needed the money for his divorce settlement.

He stopped and looked at each woman in turn with a question in his eyes.

Eve was touched by his story and felt sad for the child.

Mavis was trying to calculate the cost of repainting, as well as removing the ugly carpets.

Hilary was impressed by the wonderful kitchen breakfast and lounge area but she concealed this from Evan's gaze.

"Thank you for the tour and for the information. We will consider what you have shown us."

"But, there is much more to see," he spluttered. This was not what he expected.

"There's a finished basement with lovely features and the base of the tower is quite charming."

Mavis caught on to Hilary's plan and stood up at once, tapping Eve's hand to encourage her to follow.

They wished Evan good day and were soon back in the car and driving away. Evan stood at the front door in shock as they waved goodbye. Mavis's parting words from the car were to remind him she had his contact information. She also had a copy of the house plan taken from a display counter in the kitchen.

As soon as they were back on the road, Eve asked what had just happened.

"Is it not our Harmony House after all?"

Hilary chuckled, but Mavis replied.

"It could be, Eve, but we need to get the best possible price and it doesn't do to appear to be too eager at first."

"So this is a trick to make the poor developer lose more money as well as losing his family?"

"Don't be concerned, Eve. We do not know how much of that sad story is actually true. It wouldn't be the first time an agent has lied to potential customers."

"Did you see the horrific purple carpet on the stairs?"

"And the ghastly dark panelling in the dining room?"

"What about the lemonade walls?"

"And the art gallery misfits?"

"And the totally over-the-top tower room?"

Eve listened in confusion as the two women laughed uproariously, recalling one after another of the worst features of the home. She felt naïve for believing everything they had been told. She was especially upset at the way they mocked the fabulous pink bedroom meant for a little girl. If she had been blessed with a daughter such a place would have been her ideal. She was glad she had not made many comments. Clearly she was not as worldly as Mavis and Hilary. She decided to keep her opinions to herself and see what developed.

CHAPTER 15

Hilary knew she was playing a waiting game. Evan would contact the developer and a new price would be offered. In the meantime she and Mavis had the viewings of Camden Corners to assess and the next meeting of the women to prepare for and that involved bringing them into the picture about the possible house purchase and what the financial contribution of each member of the group might be.

To do this adequately, she sat down with Mavis to prepare a list of costings for additional changes to the Niagara house, if they managed to buy it at a reasonable price, of course.

There was also one other matter she needed to discuss with Mavis and Eve, but she postponed that one until the financial topic had been explored.

"Let's see what we would need. It can be a comprehensive list at first. We can establish priorities later and I think we should ask Eve for her opinion on the list."

Mavis had been thinking about the Niagara house ever since their visit and she was prepared with a few ideas which she wrote down on Hilary's notepad.

New paint in entrance, stairway and dining room.

Removal of panelling in dining room?

Possible change of carpeting in entrance and stairs?

Convert back stairs into elevator.

Rugs to cover white carpeting in lounge.

"Oh, you have been busy, Mavis. I like your ideas for the interior. I was also thinking of exterior requirements."

Employ gardener.

Snow removal contractor.

Check on condition of garages.

Check condition of driveway.

Talk to neighbours.

"This looks quite comprehensive. Which is the most costly?"

"The elevator is bound to be in the tens of thousands of dollars, but the fact there is a space for it is a bonus although the cost of removing the stairs first of all will add to it."

They gazed at the list and tried to estimate the costs.

"I can do a bit of painting."

"Vilma has offered to advise us on design elements."

"Perhaps the former gardener can be employed again."

"We have our own furniture and furnishings to use."

There was a silence for a minute then Hilary started to write again.

WiFi?

Security?

Nearest stores, hospital, fire department?

City Taxes?

Hydro and/or gas bills?

The two women looked at each other with the same thought in their minds. This was a very big house and a very big project. If a good bargain could not be found, it would never work.

Reality was setting in.

"Mavis, before we go any further, would you ask

Eve to come in?" I have something important to tell both of you."

Eve was in the kitchen placing a tray of muffins in the oven. She came at once and sat beside Hilary in the upstairs office.

"I apologize for not informing you about this before now but I was waiting for some further information from the police."

"What?"

Eve's face quickly lost the flush from the oven heat. She immediately suspected what was to come next.

Hilary got right to the point.

"I asked the police to investigate footprints I found in the snow leading around to the back of our house here."

"When did this happen?" Eve sounded alarmed and shaky.

Hilary turned toward her and took her hand. "It was several days ago, Eve, but I delayed telling you until I had something definite for you both. I can assure you I have been keeping an eye on the house in the evenings and watching for more footprints. The lack of fresh snow has made it difficult to track new prints but I am pretty sure he has not been around here again."

"By 'he', I presume you mean Eve's husband?"

"Correct."

"Has that been confirmed?"

"Well, not completely. The security camera showed a hooded man in dark clothes. The same man has been seen lurking in the neighbourhood and I saw him myself once, which is why I initiated a report with the police."

There was an uncomfortable silence as Hilary's listeners absorbed the impact of this announcement.

Surprisingly, it was Eve who recovered first.

"We can't be certain it was Howard. It could be someone casing the place for a break-in."

"Not reassuring, Eve!"

"Right. But we shouldn't jump to conclusions. In any case we will be out of here before too long and he won't know where we are going."

Hilary was pleased to hear Eve had developed some confidence. Knowing there were two others around and the police had been informed, had obviously given her courage.

She made a mental note to request no 'For Sale' or 'Sold' signs on the exterior. Howard, (and she, at least, was sure the interloper was Howard Dobrinski), should have no clues to follow. She would also ask Sergeant Derek Price to report on the patrol car findings and ask if those patrols might be continued until they left the district.

All of this made the coming group meeting more urgent. Decisions had to be made soon.

∼

The most urgent decision was about the Niagara house. Hilary lost no time in describing the property with the addition of the photographs. She tried to keep the doubts out of her voice but it was Mavis whose comments made the most impact on the assembled women.

"It has to be considered as a unique opportunity. We can all go there and decide afterwards what to do. As you have seen, some renovation is needed but nothing we can't afford providing we get the best possible price. Frankly, ladies, I can't see us finding a place of this size in our price bracket anywhere else in London and area."

"Well, it certainly looks interesting. I can take Jannice and Honor to see it as soon as you can set up another appointment with Evan. *He* definitely seems worth watching from his photo here!"

Vilma's comments brought laughter to the subject and Mavis went off at once to contact Evan, knowing that Hilary was all set to talk about finances as the next important step in the process.

The evening before the meeting they had a

counsel of war regarding expenses. Apart from the money each could raise from their house sales or other sources, there was the question of funding the necessary changes to the Niagara property. The paint costs would be minimal and some of that work they might be able to do by themselves, but major stuff such as replacing the back stairs with an elevator were unknown until a structural engineer surveyed the proposed location.

"I think we have to boost each person's contribution to allow for additional expenses."

Mavis had obviously given this much thought. She continued in the same vein.

"We also have to think long term. We must consider city taxes, the possible costs of a mortgage if that is the choice we make. There will also be repairs and changes that we can't know about until we take ownership."

"I see what you mean. We need a contingency fund set aside from our initial contribution and earning sufficient income to be viable when we really need the money."

There was a pause while each did mental calculations.

"Is it going to be too much for some of us?"

Hilary got out her notepad and wrote down the names.

Mavis: secure and in bank
Hilary: unknown until house sells
Vilma: secure
Eve: secure and in bank
Jannice: unknown until house sells
Honor: unknown

Two sets of eyes scanned the list.

"Not terribly certain, is it?"

"No. Too many unknowns. We need to ask Honor what her situation is. We need an electrician and an engineer to do a home inspection and most of all we need Evan to give us a good price."

"Wait one minute, Hilary. You are talking as if the other three will approve of the Niagara house. We don't know that yet."

"Of course, you are right, Mavis. Let's use the Niagara house as a test case. We'll see what the other three say about it and we could set a guide price for a contribution based on the price of the house and see what kind of a reaction we get. If someone can't meet the price it will show us what to do next."

"Do you mean we would eject a candidate at this point?"

"I know it sounds harsh. I would not want to do

that but someone might decide she couldn't proceed and voluntarily withdraw."

"I must say, I hope that is not the case. I feel we six have bonded quite nicely. But I do see the advantage in a trial run, as it were. What figure were you thinking of?"

Hilary pursed her lips and made some calculations on the page.

"One hundred forty thousand dollars each would be realistic. If Niagara does not turn out to be the house we need, we can always scale down and keep looking. We need extra time for two house sales to be completed in any case."

Mavis nodded in support. In the back of her mind she still worried about getting Eve away from the area to a new location as quickly as possible.

When Hilary announced the provisional contribution sum, Mavis watched to see the reactions among the group.

Vilma reached over to Jannice and patted her hand reassuringly, with a smile that said, 'We'll be OK'.

Honor looked down at her folded hands and then up at Hilary with what Mavis interpreted as a look of decision.

Eve looked anxiously from one face to another. In her heart she saw them all safely living together at the Niagara house and she feared that dream might not come to pass.

Hilary waited for another moment for a negative reaction and when none appeared she sighed in satisfaction.

Mavis jumped in with the good news. "Evan says we can go to view the house again tomorrow if that suits everyone."

Expressions of delight circulated around the room and Eve went off to refill the tea cups. Vilma volunteered to be the driver and a time for the viewing appointment was discussed.

CHAPTER 16

Evan Mahavolich was feeling optimistic about the second viewing. Prior to his clients' arrival, he went around the whole house figuring out what to say about each room to give the best impression. In his pocket he had a price from the seller but it was his business to ensure that bottom-line price was not used if at all possible. Still, the seller was keen to be shot of what he thought of as a white elephant.

It could turn out to be a win/win for the agent.

Evan was most worried about the tall woman who had been so negative before. He must show her something to change her perspective. Possibly the basement which they had not seen before she left?

Possibly, the base of the tower room which was definitely multi-purpose, depending on needs?

He had asked a painter and decorator to look at the entrance and main staircase and provide an estimate. The re-painting price was reasonable, but removing and replacing that awful carpet was going to be expensive. And that did not include removing the panelling in the dining room.

He was wondering if a dye job would reduce the impact of the stair carpet when the car arrived in the side driveway and three different women emerged from it.

His first emotion was relief. The tall angry one was not in this group but he spotted the leader the minute she got out of the driver's seat of the expensive car and headed right for him. She was good looking, wearing beautiful clothes and boots and had jewellery that even his amateur gaze identified as real gems.

She advanced with outstretched hand and confidently declared her intention.

"Good to meet you, Evan. Show us what you've got here. We two want the full tour but Honor will stay mainly on the ground level unless you can show her an easy access to the basement?"

At once he was given a challenge and knew he was in the presence of a master manipulator who already knew all the tricks of the trade. He wondered if she had been a real estate agent at some time in her life.

He quickly did the main level spiel and as the two women advanced up the stairway, he conducted the lady with the walking stick back outside to the wraparound porch from which there was direct access to the basement level door, down only three wide steps with railings on either side.

Honor was pleased to be the one who was seeing the basement for the first time. 'Basement' was not a correct description for what she now saw. The entire area was fully finished in neutral tones and consisted of what appeared to be a separate, open-plan apartment, complete with kitchen and sliding door exit to the paved area of the back yard. A laundry and furnace room were concealed in one rear corner and the opposite corner consisted of storage space already supplied with shelving. The enclosed bedroom and washroom occupied the middle area. The remaining floor space was big enough for a gym as well as an office.

Honor had been given the job of keeping Evan occupied while Vilma did some measurements upstairs.

"So, Evan, what are the chances of getting

internet access and Wi-Fi services out here on the fringes of London?"

"Well, the builder assures me everything is set up for all the technology required. Were you thinking of setting up a business here?"

"It's a possibility, among others." She wandered back to the full washroom with the rain shower and interior bench seat. He followed.

"May I ask if your friends today are involved with Mrs. Dempster who made the initial enquiry?"

He was clearly trying to estimate what the situation was here. Two families or two sets of friends or two entirely different groups of potential buyers. Honor had been instructed to keep him guessing.

"Could you demonstrate how these folding doors operate? I would like to see the size of the patio."

He rushed to unlock the system so that the doors slid easily into a concertina shape against one wall.

"In summer, it's open to the outside so the patio becomes a part of the main house for parties and entertaining."

"A lovely feature, Evan. What about security?"

He went into a prepared speech about the builder adding various safety features because he and his family intended to travel during the winter months. By the time he had finished, Honor was sure the rest of the group had seen everything they needed to.

"Well, then, Evan, it all sounds satisfactory. Let's join the others now. You can lock up here."

When they returned to the front entrance, Vilma and Jannice were waiting.

"Thank you so much Evan. We may be in touch soon. Have a good day, now. Bye."

With that they departed for the side driveway and the car, and he was left standing at the door with his mouth hanging open. This was going to make a good story when he got back to the office but whether or not it would result in a good sale, well that was another matter altogether. He was not looking forward to his conversation with the builder, or with the builder's wife.

Vilma Smith drove to the nearest Tim Horton's in Colonel Talbot Road and chose a quiet table in the far corner where they could talk freely over coffee, soup, sandwiches and doughnuts.

"All right everyone! Let's compare notes. Honor, you first."

"I must say, the lower level is amazing! It's virtually a one bedroom apartment and the view plus the access to the backyard are both superb. It could be turned into anything we might need."

"So, definitely another bedroom then?"

"Absolutely, and lots more besides!"

"Am I right? That makes a total of five bedrooms upstairs and one more in the lower level."

"Don't forget the tower room on the ground floor. It's a kind of library at the moment but could easily be a seventh bedroom."

"Or a television room."

"Or a dining room. I hate that other dark one."

"Or a music room. I would love to have a piano."

"Hold on a minute before you have us all moved into the place! Does this mean we three support the Niagara house as a suitable home for all of us?"

A chorus of 'Yes!" was the response. It was so enthusiastic that several patrons looked up from their coffee and conversation to see if a riot was taking shape at the corner table. All they could see was a trio of women smiling and toasting each other with coffee cups.

Jannice was enthralled. "I have never even seen such a beautiful house before. To think of actually living there with you lovely women is more than a dream come true for me. I am afraid to hope, just in case it doesn't come true."

Vilma was aware that most of Jannice's dreams had been shattered by her family responsibilities and she made a silent promise to do anything she could to turn that streak of bad luck around before it was too late.

Honor had remained practical. "I suppose there are more things than sleeping quarters to consider. What about the elevator idea? That one could be important for all of us for one reason or another."

"You are so right," responded Jannice." How I wish I had one when my mother and father were having such trouble climbing stairs. I almost fell more than once when trying to lift them from step to step."

"It's a huge advantage, Honor and Jannice. I think the measurements will work and from the plans Mavis brought back, I believe access to the laundry room would be where the elevator ends No carrying heavy loads up and down stairs."

She made a mental note to ask if an elevator could have an entry point at ground level as well as access on the top floor and the basement.

All three stopped to think of the advantages of living in the Niagara house. They realized there were decisions to be made that might test their present camaraderie but each one was prepared to make compromises if it meant they had the chance to walk freely in and out of that huge home and live there securely for as long as they wished.

Hilary was eagerly waiting at home to hear the decision. When she saw their faces she knew at once the feeling was unanimous. Now it was all up to the negotiations with Evan. She felt they had kept him guessing and he would pass on that message to his client. She made no announcement yet, but she thought that soon they would have to begin calling it Harmony House instead of Niagara house.

CHAPTER 17

Immediately after their visit to the Niagara house, Vilma and Jannice went into high gear. Everything depended on getting a good price for Jannice's house. Vilma, a lifelong newspaper reader, arrived the next morning waving two pieces of news from the daily paper. The first was the information that in order to celebrate Canada's 150th birthday, Museum London would soon provide a free appraisal opportunity for heirlooms, antiques and collectibles.

"But I wouldn't know what was valuable and what was trash," moaned Jannine.

"Well, we would need to be judicious about what we present. We could go with a set of something like silver or pottery, rather than one single item which might be worthless in today's antique markets. There's also the advantage to be gained by observing what others bring in to be evaluated. We could listen into what's being said and get some idea of what to look for. The paper says twenty London area museums, heritage sites and organizations will also give talks. We will definitely collect business cards for future contact."

"You are so smart, Vilma."

"Nonsense! I have had more experience, that's all. Now, we need to scour the basement and the attic to make sure we don't miss something that might be valuable. We don't have much time left before the big day and we must reserve a time slot if we want to be sure to get the attention of professionals."

Most of the worst rubbish had already gone via the Junk Removal men so it was not too difficult to identify the remaining places to search through. Vilma had not yet seen anything remarkable. The fine china was not saleable any more. No one in the younger generations wanted dishes that could not be tossed into a dishwasher. Most silver services from previous generations were not pure silver but a coating of silver plating and worth nothing to collectors. She feared Jannice would be lucky to uncover one item of value but, the chances were, there was nothing here at all.

She sent Jannice up to pull down the attic steps and try to find something. First, she warned her to take a torch and to cover her hair in case droppings from rodents were in the rafters. Jannice took the warning seriously and climbed up wearing a coat and rubber boots and a wide-brimmed summer hat. She said, to her knowledge, no person had dared to climb into the attic in many decades.

In the meantime, Vilma re-read the second newspaper clipping which stated Old East London could be the site of another massive highrise apartment development such as had been springing up rapidly in downtown London in recent years.

There was a quote in the article from Ian Stone, head of Paramount Developments.

"The neighbourhood is changing. It will be a chic, happening place with theatre and arts.

We have a lot of confidence in that area."

There was nothing concrete in the article with regard to planning permission, so the time frame was not clear but she thought it was a likely incentive as far as estate agents were concerned. She decided to drive along Jannice's street on her way home, looking for other properties for sale. A joint proposition could draw interest if others were thinking of selling. She thought an enquiry flyer to that end might be dropped into a few mailboxes as well.

She was doing some preliminary thinking about the flyer when she heard a very loud noise from above.

Lord! I hope I was wrong about rodents.

She ran upstairs and climbed up the ladder to the attic so she could look inside, praying all the while that she wouldn't see Jannice flat on her back in a cloud of spider webs and dust.

"Are you all right?"

"Sorry for the loud bang. I knocked over a stack of boxes and thought they were going to go right through the flooring. I am fine but I don't think I can move the boxes again. They are very heavy."

"Don't strain your back. What's in them?"

"I have no idea. There's nothing written on the outside that I can see. Probably more old kitchen junk.

Should I try to open one?"

"It's likely to be books. Some old encyclopedia sets, I imagine. They are the heaviest items. Don't bother, Jannice. Take a look around to see if there's anything else of interest and come down. You've already stirred up enough dust."

Vilma carefully descended the ladder and went straight to the washroom to wash her hands and brush her hair. She had a deathly fear of spiders from the time in her childhood when her youngest brother had shoved one down the neck of her school blouse. The dirty, dark attic was exactly where spiders preferred to live.

By the time she reached the kitchen again, it seemed so much brighter and welcoming by contrast. She put on the kettle for tea and reminded herself to check Jannice for insects, dead or alive as soon as she emerged.

She was back at the flyer idea and on her second cup before she noticed the time had passed and still no sign of Jannice. There had not been any further worrying noises, so she got up to go and see what was delaying her.

As she reached the bottom of the stairs to the second floor she stopped short and gasped. A ghostly figure was coming toward her, swathed in long delicate fabric covering arms and legs completely and with a huge cartwheel of a hat concealing the face, heavy with flowers and veils and trailing vines.

What came to mind was Dickens' woeful Miss Haversham, frozen in time and still adorned in her wedding finery.

"What do you think, Vilma?"

It was a jolt of relief to recognize Jannice's voice emerging from beneath the hat.

"I found these in an old wardrobe in a corner behind the box pile. There was a key in the lock and sheets over top of the outfits so they are in good shape, I think. This is gorgeous! So ladylike, don't you agree?

I had no clue anything like this was in the house."

Vilma had recovered her breath enough to jump start her brain.

"Be careful on the stairs. Don't trip over that skirt."

She stretched out her hand to help Jannice down to the floor level, all the while examining the quality of the materials and the embroidery that decorated them. Her mind was reeling with ideas. This was a genuine outfit from a prior era and seemed to be intact. Eldon House in London would adore having something like this for their docents who conducted tours in the Harris home. Film companies or Theatre London would compete for the authentic items she saw before her. Historical television shows like Downton Abbey would save a fortune by using real items instead of having to recreate them in inferior materials.

"You haven't said anything, Vilma. Don't you like this? Are you annoyed with me for wasting time?"

She gulped. The vision of competing buyers was still in the forefront of her mind.

"Is there more up there?"

"I didn't disturb the rest but the wardrobe looks full, as far as I could see. Why?"

"This dress you are wearing is beautiful. It is hand-embroidered and the material is in great condition. If the other items in the wardrobe are of a similar standard you might well have found our treasures for the Museum experts."

"Really?"

"We'll have to figure out a way to display the outfits. This dress fits you very well, Jannice. We could take a series of photographs of you in the outfits and take a sample of the materials with us to show the quality. I very much doubt anyone else will have such a thing to show off. It could be exactly what we need to boost the price of the house. I would make the photos and the story available to the London Free Press. It could garner a lot of attention. Do you have any idea how these clothes came to be in the attic?"

"No. I never heard anyone talk about clothes. Who would have packed them up so carefully? It was beyond my parents to even get up there in their later years. Does it matter?"

"If there's a connection with a specific family or

person of note in London, it definitely makes the clothes more desirable. I think we're going to have to search that wardrobe for information, but first, please let me help you take that gorgeous dress off. If you rip a tear in the skirt we could never repair it properly."

Jannice had simply put the dress over her head without fastening the row of tiny buttons that ran from the lace collar to below the waistline. Vilma removed the hat and placed it carefully on the kitchen table. The flowers were also hand-made of ribbon and sewn onto the brim. There was a long lace ribbon attached to the crown, meant to anchor the hat to a lady's hairstyle. The workmanship was exquisite.

As soon as the dress had been carefully removed, Vilma took it up in her arms and examined the neckline. As she had hoped, there was an embroidered satin label stitched in place with the name of the seamstress and, glory be!, the name of the woman who had ordered it.

A unique Kingsmill's design made for Mrs. Jordan O'Connor.

"The clothes are legitimately yours, Jannice! Someone in your family presumably ordered this dress and the chances are good everything in the wardrobe upstairs belonged to the same woman."

"But they are so delicate and expensive looking. Who would have worn this? Where would it be worn? What occasion? Where would this kind of money come from?"

"We'll have to dig out some of those answers, but we have a place to start now and if you are up to it, let's go back to the attic and see what else is in that wardrobe."

Hilary had a call from her real estate agent early the next morning after the meeting. She took the call in her office where she had gone to read over her costings for the proposed Harmony House.

She listened intently for a minute or two and made a few notes on her notepad but did not commit to a definite yes or no. The offers required some thought and she was glad to be able to sit quietly and work out what was best.

She found it strange to be contemplating two house price negotiations at the same time. Ethan had submitted his developer's final selling price of

$700,000 which reflected the clever way the women had approached the Niagara house's deficits. The price was better than she had expected and would give the women some wiggle room with regard to future improvements.

For her own financial situation, she was pleased to see two bids of roughly similar levels. Clearly, the Fanshawe College offer was preferable but the other bidder was from the Toronto area. This move away from the huge city was a growing trend for retired Torontonians. The couple were anxious to move soon and had finances in place. Fanshawe could take a long time to close the deal as they were heavily invested in the Dundas Street store presently being converted to meet their needs for a new, downtown, hi-tech training facility.

She wondered if she could put a little more pressure on the second bid, given that the college was still interested. No sooner had this thought occurred than Hilary chastised herself for being greedy. She would easily get her $140,000 for her home and the deal on the future Harmony House was already a bargain. No point in risking trouble by asking too much from fate. Whoever the new owners of 46, Camden Corners were, they could deal with Fanshawe College if they wished. Hilary Dempster had more than enough on her plate.

She made a note to start the search for a well-known, reliable lawyer and financial advisor and to look for a structural engineering firm to advise about the elevator installation. If that major item could be done first, the moving into Harmony House would be much easier for everyone.

Harmony House.

It was, hopefully, a propitious name. Many cultures believe a good name brings good fortune. So far it was proving to be true.

Mavis remembered Vilma talking about the lawyer who handled her inheritance issues. She gave her phone a call and found her at Jannice's preparing the house for sale.

"Oh, I recommend Jeffrey highly. He's the scion of a well-respected London family business. He would handle everything discreetly and promptly. If you like, I will give him a call and set up an appointment.

And while I am thinking of it...... should we throw poor Ethan a bone and ask him to sell Jannice's house?"

Mavis chuckled. "I don't see why not. That goes for both of your suggestions Vilma! Would you be comfortable attending the appointment with us?"

"Of course! I'll be in touch with the date and time."

Hilary had already begun to search the phone book's yellow pages for an engineer to tackle the elevator problem. She found plenty ads for the stair lifts that promised 'one-day installation' but nothing of the scope of their project. Mavis assured her there was time to find a suitable firm as the final papers for the sale of the Niagara house had not yet been signed.

"Yes, about that. We will need a sizable deposit to hold the house. At the moment we only have access to your money and Eve's. I can add a few thousands to that sum and I am sure Vilma would forward some of hers but I am reluctant to take their money until an official transfer can be authorized by the banks in question. Every single thing from here on, needs to be done with the ultimate in security for our partners. All of us must have complete confidence in the process. That means ironclad contracts.

I hope Vilma gets that appointment soon. Handling this amount of money makes me nervous."

To Hilary's surprise it was Honor who found the engineer. She used an elevator every day in her apartment building and she made note of the firm that inspected the equipment on a regular basis.

She had even met one of the employees on a day when the elevator was out of order. He was kind enough to carry her wheelchair downstairs for her so she could go out, and she knew the man's name.

"I remember him because of his consideration and also because his name was easily confused with mine. He was called Jared Place. We laughed about it. I'll get the building superintendent to call and see if we can employ him and his company."

Every little bit of help was welcomed by Mavis and Hilary. It meant they were no longer alone in making important decisions. The more each person in the group participated, the better their long-term success would be.

"It's good that we all have an equal stake in this project succeeding. It reminds me of the most effective school staffs I worked with. When everyone has a voice there are fewer complaints and concerns unexpressed and liable to breed discontent."

"I never thought of it that way, Hilary, but I suppose every business works best with cooperation among employees. It certainly applied to my job at the courthouse. We must make sure every one of us has an important role to play right from the beginning. Is there anyone you are concerned about?"

"I suppose Eve is the one who has the least to offer."

"I disagree, Hilary. She is gradually coming out of her shell. She does a lot of the kitchen work and I know she wants to be a full member of the team. I think she would make a great 'house mother' to keep us all in order. A kind of communications person; she has a sweet personality."

"I didn't mean to sound disparaging, Mavis. You are right, of course. I haven't spent as much time with Eve as you have."

"There's been a lot on your mind, Hilary, but I am hopeful things will smooth out soon. We are well on our way."

CHAPTER 18

Sometimes, when everything seems the most blocked, one item breaks the impasse and forward progress begins to flow in a more normal fashion again.

The visit to Vilma's lawyer was that item for the Harmony House group.

In only a matter of minutes, Jeffrey Thomas laid out a series of actions to move their house purchase along rapidly. He had already been in contact with Evan and the developer and secured the house transfer which would be done formally in the Thomas Andersen Pitman offices within a week.

"The developer chappie would have liked the entire purchase price up front but I declared that suggestion was totally unrealistic, and substituted a payment schedule starting with a down payment of 10% on signing."

Hilary could feel her tension evaporating with every word from the mouth of Jeffrey Thomas. He was an older gentleman wearing a navy suit and waistcoat and a tie she knew belonged to the London Hunt Club. He was shaved and combed and his grey hair was slicked back with a touch of pomade in the old style. She recognized the scent as one her father once used.

Further confidence was established as soon as she observed the manner in which he greeted Vilma; like an old friend but with respect. He shook her hand and attended to her introductions as was proved by the fact he called Mavis and Hilary by the correct names.

"Mrs. Dempster, I believe I played golf with your husband several times. He was a fine player. Many were sad at his early demise. My sympathies to you, and to your family. Is Desmond back in town?"

"Thank you for your kindness. No, Desmond is still working in Toronto. I don't see him very often these days."

The tone for the meeting was set and Mr. Thomas proceeded to advance through the legal requirements commending Mavis and Hilary for the groundwork they had provided.

"I have consulted a colleague in Bracebridge who put me in touch with Shelley Raymond, president of Solterra Co-housing. I now have the details of Ontario legislation concerning building codes, provincial and municipal legislation and human rights laws. I can assure you everything will be done in accord with these regulations. You need have no worries about that."

He turned some papers over and checked his computer screen before continuing.

Mavis and Hilary had just enough time to mouth 'Thank God!' to each other. Vilma caught this and smiled contentedly. She was happy to have steered them to the right place and especially to the right person.

"With respect to the down payment; I recommend a bank order from each person who will be contributing. Divide the $70,000 equally and I will have receipts notarized as soon as the cheques are handed over. This will give you access to the property for inspections and any improvements you wish to make. I know this is a new build but I suggest an engineer be employed to do a thorough inspection of the footings and the roof, and the mechanical room. I have taken the liberty of asking a local company with which I have had successful dealings, to do this task for you. Here is the card. He will report to me when his inspection is complete and the cost will come from my fee."

Hilary was emboldened by his obvious efficiency and asked his opinion of the company Honor had mentioned for the elevator installation.

"The elevator is an excellent idea, which will reduce your insurance premiums. The company has installed most of the elevators in London highrise buildings which speaks well of their reputation. Let me see the bill for the work and I will have someone review it and also supervise the actual work for you."

Mavis felt as if a weighty cloak of worry had fallen from her shoulders. She spoke up on behalf of her friend, in the knowledge that Hilary felt the same.

"Mr.Thomas, I can't tell you how relieved we feel to have you advise us so competently. You have given our project much thought and we are tremendously grateful to you for your work on our behalf."

The three women emerged from the offices of Thomas, Andersen and Pitman into a day of dazzling brightness that perfectly matched their feelings. There was a new light covering of snow on the ground, and they were standing near the outdoor skating rink of Covent Garden Market with lunchtime skaters whizzing around mothers whose children were dressed in bright colours. Sounds of carefree laughter rose into the cold air.

"Look, we have to go through the market building to get our cars from the parking levels, why don't we make a morning of it and have fresh-ground coffee here with bagels or sandwiches prepared to order."

"Wonderful idea, Vilma! We could buy some fresh vegetables from the stalls and a celebration cake for later and isn't there a cheese stand with selections from all over the world?"

"You two are exactly right. It's time for a treat. I'm for some of those special chocolates and fresh bread, although not meant to be eaten together."

Hilary's agreement brought them all to a relieved laughter and they paused to enjoy the scene in front of them before entering the doors to the warm inside of the market building, replete with many delicious aromas of food, flowers and coffee. They wandered about through the lines of stalls commenting on the produce before making their lunch selections and finding a table near the entrance. The only requirement for the rest of the day was to bring the good news to Honor, Jannice and Eve.

"I'll tell Jannice. I am expected at her house this afternoon."

Vilma then told Mavis and Hilary of the discovery of an entire wardrobe full of exquisite clothing in Jannice's attic. In a day of good news this was the icing on the cake.

"And you have no idea how it got there?"

"I believe it's a trousseau, meant for a wealthy lady. None of it is worn. Jannice was completely astonished at finding it. She estimates it's much older than the house so we will have to go back in her family history to discover the story."

"That's amazing! I can't wait to hear what the experts say about it. You mentioned that Jannice has decided to dress up in the outfits?"

"Yes! She's the right size, unbelievably. I contacted a wedding photographer and he has agreed to come to the house to do the work. I don't want to risk moving the clothing."

"It sounds like a perfect advert for the house sale; 'A House with a History'."

Vilma had not thought this far but Mavis's suggestion made good sense.

Once all the food had been consumed and the shopping completed, Hilary decided to go by taxi to Honor's apartment and tell her the good news. Mavis knew she wanted to have a private conversation with the younger woman about her finances and now that the house purchase was secured, it was a good time to find out if Honor was able to participate fully.

Mavis would drive home to Camden Corners with the groceries and tell Eve all about their meeting with Jeffrey Thomas.

Mavis hardly noticed the traffic she was so excited by the morning's events. She was planning to fix a lovely lunch for Eve since she had missed the treats the others had shared. She parked the car in the driveway and carried the fancy cream cake in its box carefully up the front steps and into the house, after negotiating the lock and balancing the cake box in her other hand. She would collect the rest of the shopping once the cake was safely delivered to the kitchen counter.

The house was silent. She felt a tiny disappointment not to see Eve in the kitchen. All the way home, she had been planning to reveal the good news to her over a cup of hot tea. Eve must be busy upstairs.

She hung up her coat and hat and dropped her purse on the counter next to the cake box. With a happy smile she reached into the cutlery drawer and withdrew the spade-shaped cake slicer, placing it ready to use beside the cake box. She was about to call out for Eve when something caught her eye.

There was a clump of snow in the hallway leading to the stairs. It was beginning to melt leaving a puddle. She knew she had not gone beyond the kitchen in her winter boots. There should not be snow in the house. She removed her boots and checked the soles. She had wiped them on the mat inside the door and they were damp but clean.

Suddenly the silence became fraught with danger. Where was Eve? Why had she not come downstairs when she heard the front door opening?

Her heart missed a beat. *Howard Dobrinski!*

A chill that had nothing to do with the temperature, settled on her body. The possibility of an intruder....*a known intruder, a violent man,* brought a jolt of fear which focussed her mind immediately.

Eve must be upstairs right now with that man who had beaten her badly before this, without the reasons he now thought he had.

Her body said, 'flee from danger' but her mind took control. She turned and tiptoed into the kitchen. Beside the wall phone there was a cork bulletin board where messages were pinned. She lifted the phone in a shaking hand and searched for the card Hilary had brought from the police station with the name of the Sergeant who knew her from schooldays.

There it was. Derek Price. She carefully dialed the number and prayed it would be answered at once. She swallowed to bring moisture back to her dry mouth as she waited, counting the rings. She had no idea what she would do if an answer phone took over the call. She needed help and quickly. Anything could be happening to Eve.

A male voice on the line said, "Sergeant Price, how can I assist you?"

She whispered the words that came first to her mind.

"I need help right now at Hilary's. An intruder. He's..."

A rough, large hand clamped around her neck cutting off her voice. The phone dropped from her hand and clanged against the wall. He picked it up and returned it without saying a word.

Mavis Montgomery knew who her assailant was. She had never seen the man but she knew it was Howard Dobrinski.

Through her terror she wished she had left the house immediately to get help but at the same time she could not have left Eve alone with this evil creature who had stalked his wife until he knew her location and knew the habits of the other house occupants. He had waited until she was the only one inside. And now he had two captives in his control. Hilary was not expected for an hour at least. The police call was interrupted before she could explain the situation.

He tightened the grip around her throat and dragged her to the staircase. She tried to pull back from him but her foot slipped on the wet floor and she went down, hitting her forehead on a riser. He pulled her upright immediately but she was so dazed she could hardly function.

"Well, now, aren't you the feisty one! Which one are you? Let's go up and see what Eve has to say about you."

The voice was deep and dark. She caught a whiff of stale beer as he dragged her bodily up the stairs bumping her legs on one after another of the stairs until they reached the top. The pain brought her back to full consciousness. She knew she had to try to think clearly before he did something to remove her options.

The door to Mavis and Eve's room stood open. Mavis twisted her head to see inside. Eve was tied to the bed frame by her wrists. There was a wad of cloth stuck inside her mouth but her eyes signalled fear and distress as soon as she saw Mavis.

Dobrinski threw Mavis down on the second bed

and turned to rummage in a drawer for something to tie her up with. She had gone limp when she saw Eve so she had only a few moments before he realized she was fully conscious.

Her mind raced faster than ever before in her life. What was in a bedroom that could be used against this large, powerful man? What could she reach quickly?

He was mouthing obscenities as he threw female underwear onto the floor in his search for less flimsy materials. She had only seconds to act decisively. She forced down panic and spared a second to glance over to Eve in the vain hope of reassuring her. Eve's eyes were frantically looking upward, flicking up as far as her head could move. Was she having a seizure? Mavis's eyes followed automatically and she saw what Eve meant. On the wall above each bed was a framed print of ferns. The pictures were large, in a heavy wooden frame and glassed.

Without a clear idea of what she would do, she stood up on the bed, steadied herself against the wall and lifted off the picture.

He had now found a sock drawer in the bottom of a dresser. He was on his knees pulling out short socks to find those long enough to tie around wrists and ankles.

Mavis never knew how she had the strength but she found it somewhere.

The crash of breaking glass was like a vehicle collision. He dropped sideways to the floor, covered in glass fragments and bits of the wooden frame. There was blood on the back of his head but she only remembered that much later.

She ran to Eve, pulled out the wad of cloth, and began to untie her hands. Eve gasped for air and saliva again, but as soon as Mavis released one hand she tore at the other and ordered Mavis to get the door key from the china dish on top of the dresser. This required Mavis to walk around the prone figure of Howard Dobrinski but she did it, shuddering all the while, grabbed the key, and was pushed out the door into the hallway by a frantic Eve who locked the door at once and continued down the stairs with Mavis in tow.

"We have to get away," she cried. "He could wake up at any moment. He swore he was going to kill me. We have to get help. *Now!*"

Eve flung open the front door and ran outside down the steps in bare feet with Mavis following. As the snow hit her stocking feet she came back to sanity and looked around for the nearest neighbour who might be at home. The women could not run for long in this condition, in the cold. She ran forward to stop Eve without a clear idea of what to do next when a harsh sound caused her to look up.

Speeding along the street with sirens blaring was a police cruiser.

Thank God! Mavis simply collapsed where she stood. All strength left her at the sight of rescue.

Eve continued to run until she reached the vehicle which stopped just in time to avoid hitting her.

Mavis vaguely remembered hearing voices. Eve's high-pitched and frantic. Male voices questioning and reassuring. The next thing she was aware of was a policewoman's warm hands helping her up and taking her into her own car still standing in the driveway.

"You're safe now. We'll wait here until the officers can assess the situation inside the house. Your friend is with them. They will take care of her."

A blanket was produced from the rear seat and wrapped around Mavis. She clutched at it. Her teeth were chattering together as the shock hit. She and Eve could have been killed by that................ No word bad enough to describe her feelings presented itself.

Unrelated thoughts crowded her mind. Where were her boots? Did she turn the kettle off? Who was going to pick the broken glass off the carpet upstairs? Why did her head hurt so much?

She unwrapped one hand and touched her forehead. A lump was already forming.

The policewoman saw the gesture and said, "We'll get you checked out by the hospital, don't worry. Your friend will come too. When you feel better you can give me the number of someone to call who can look after you both."

Hospital?

Hilary?

Lord above, Hilary must not return home and find this chaos.

The calm, soothing voice of the policewoman continued.

"Now, I want you to stay safe with me. Officers are bringing the man out of the house. An ambulance has been called and I will stay with you and your friend. Do you know where the keys are so we can lock up the house? No one else should enter until evidence has been gathered."

Mavis had to focus on the question but as soon as she tried to retrace her actions on first returning home, her mind sheered away from the moment of the attack and fixed instead on the cake slicer she had left on the countertop.

"Purse. Kitchen."

"That's fine. In a few minutes I will go inside and get your friend and the keys, then we'll all go to the hospital together. Is it all right if I look for your coats and your boots?"

Nodding was not a good idea. Mavis tried to smile but feared a grimace was all she managed. She clung onto the woman's arm not wanting to be left alone. Eventually the need to see how Eve was surviving overcame her reluctance and she murmured something about being 'fine now'. Fine was a condition she could not even visualize at this moment. It was like a far off mountaintop.

The policewoman patted her shoulder and went off up the front steps and the reality of the situation began to get through the cold, immobile part of Mavis Montgomery's brain.

CHAPTER 19

Hilary and Honor had a good chat about future plans. Honor was honest about her situation and she actually produced a printed spreadsheet outlining how her finances would come together in the next few weeks. Hilary was impressed. She was also impressed by the office area in the small apartment which Honor showed her. The second bedroom was devoted to her business and the entire room was set up for the purpose and arranged in such a way that Hilary could see how efficient and organized this young woman was. From the computers, there were two, to the shelves on which colour-coded files stood at the ready, to the high-tech printer/ fax/ copier, everything spoke of Honor Pace's abilities in the field of internet business skills. The bright red hair was not, it seemed, indicative of her reliability.

As Hilary had just come from the lawyer's office and now knew the kind of complications that lay ahead for the co-housing project, she felt relieved to know they would have a competent internet person installed in Harmony House.

"Oh, Honor, thanks again for the suggestion about the elevator company. It looks like we will go ahead with them. That reminds me to ask about your impressions of the lower level of Harmony House. I am thinking it would be the perfect location for you."

"I hardly dare ask for that prime spot, Hilary. It is more than I need. Could I request it temporarily, until I am fully mobile again? Access to that amazing patio and garden must be available for all our house members to enjoy in the better weather."

"That sounds reasonable, but I feel the space you need for your business fits the area well as long as you are content with being interrupted every time someone uses the laundry or sits outside chatting over a cup of coffee."

"Truthfully, I would be glad of the interruptions. I am tired of living alone like this. My business doesn't occupy my entire day and one of my reasons for seeking out your group is my desire for the company of like-minded women."

Hilary chuckled. "I think we can supply the company you want. We'll consider the lower area yours for now and the next step to make it easily available for the rest of us will be worked out later."

They were celebrating this mutually-beneficial decision over tea and cookies when Hilary's phone began to chime its carillion.

"Excuse me for one moment, Honor."

She removed the phone from its designated pocket in her purse and answered in a cheery voice without looking to see where the call was coming from.

"Hello."

"Hilary Montgomery?"

"Yes. Who's calling this number?"

"I am a police officer calling on behalf of Mavis Montgomery and Eve Dobrinski."

"What's happened?"

"Your friends are fine now. They are at London Health Sciences' Emergency where they have been checked out by doctors and declared ready to be released."

"Was there an accident?"

"There was a home invasion and I need to ask if you

could take your friends to a hotel or another house for a night. Your house is the scene of a crime and access needs to be restricted for twenty-four hours."

Hilary stopped and took a deep breath. Honor saw her face blanch and knew there was trouble.

"I will find somewhere. Are you sure Mavis and Eve are well? Can I come now? Will you fill me in on the details?"

"Yes, to everything you ask. An officer will be with your friends and he will tell you what occurred. When can you be here?"

"Soon. I am not far away. Please tell them I am coming."

"Of course."

The call ended. Honor waited in suspense. Hilary gathered her courage.

"There's been some kind of break-in at my home. Mavis and Eve are in hospital but they have recovered. I don't know for sure but my instinct tells me it has something to do with Eve's Howard Dobrinski.

I need to find a place for us for tonight until the police are finished at the house."

Honor quickly grasped the situation. "Would Vilma be able to take you three for the night? It would be better if you were with a friend rather than in an impersonal hotel. I will track Vilma down for you and alert her."

Hilary was already pulling on her coat.

"Excellent idea! You know my number. Let me know if Vilma can do it."

Before Hilary reached her car, Honor had found Vilma and filled her in with the little she knew.

"I'm leaving Jannice's now. Tell Hilary to bring them to me. I'll get everything ready for them.

Thanks Honor. I'll call you once they are settled."

Hilary Dempster broke her own rules by speeding to the hospital. If anyone had dared to stop her she was ready with her excuse. This was an emergency.

She parked in the nearest spot to the entrance without bothering to check if it was permitted. Then she ran at full tilt for the double doors which separated as soon as she approached. Into her mind came Mavis's account of waiting in this same place when Eve was there. This time, Hilary decided she was not going to wait. She needed to see Mavis and Eve at once.

Calming herself, but fully aware she was using her most authoritative voice and manner, she spoke urgently to the person behind the glass window and explained that she had been instructed *by the police* to come and fetch her friends, Mavis Montgomery and Eve Dobrinski.

Apparently, she was expected. A young doctor was summoned and he took her to a waiting room where the two women sat silently together with their arms linked. She saw a large bruise on Mavis's forehead and asked about it.

"The doctor checked my reactions. He said I have a slight concussion but it will be fine if I take it easy for a few days."

"Oh, Mavis!"

"She was so brave, Hilary. She saved my life. I don't know what I would have done......."

"Say no more now, let's get out of here. I need to talk to the officer then we'll go to Vilma's for the night."

The officer was at a table conferring with the doctor on duty. Hilary identified herself and he drew her aside so no one could hear their conversation.

"It's safe to say Mr. Dobrinski is under remand for ignoring a harassment order and assaulting his wife and her friend. Sergeant Price asked me to tell you there is no possibility of bail. He will be held until the judge can appoint a solicitor. We have two witnesses and a prior complaint, as well as evidence now being gathered. We will contact you some time tomorrow when we are ready to release the house back to you."

"Thank you, officer. I don't know what else to say. I am still in shock."

"Drive carefully then."

"I will."

He shook her hand and at that moment her phone beeped. She saw the text message from Honor and was glad Honor had also thought to provide the directions to Vilma's house. In her present distracted mental state Hilary was not sure she could find her way out of the hospital without help.

Vilma would look after all three of them, she knew. For once, Hilary Dempster was happy to relinquish responsibility. She would drive carefully to Vilma's and help to look after the victims but she was not sure she would be able to sleep this night.

Vilma Smith's home was brightly lit, warm inside and full of all the comforts any person could wish for.

As soon as she saw the three bedraggled women emerge from the car, she knew not to ask any questions but to provide all the hot food and drink they needed and to show them to the bedrooms she had prepared. She put Hilary in a twin room with Mavis and installed Eve in a single room right next to her own with a door left open between them. The lights would stay on all night and she would set out snacks and drinks in the kitchen should anyone find it difficult to sleep.

Mavis had headache medication and Eve had been provided with a mild sedative by the doctor. If they preferred, she was satisfied if they wished to stay comfortably by the fireside all night. She had a stack of soft blankets and throws there as well as pillows. There was a television above the fireplace and quiet classical music to distract them if they wanted it.

Hilary drew Vilma aside when she saw all the preparations that had been made.

"I am so grateful you were standing by, Vilma. This is a shocking business. I don't know if I could have coped on my own tonight."

"Don't mention it. I have had enough drama in my life to know how important it is to have friends to call upon when they are needed. Make yourself at home, Hilary. You are not alone in this. We will sort it out together. We are all strong women here."

"All I can think of is how fast I can sell my home now. It's tainted forever and I will never feel the same way about it."

"Don't worry about the future. We are safe here for now and you can stay as long as you need. I will call Jannice and Honor and tell them everyone is cared for."

Hilary went back to the fireside where Mavis and Eve had settled. She clung to the thought this awful event might have one good outcome. If this crisis did not bind all six women together into a mutually-supportive family group, nothing ever would.

CHAPTER 20

Surprising to Hilary, she slept well in Vilma's lovely second bedroom. When she looked over to the twin bed she saw it had not been slept in. She decided to have a hot shower to wash away the previous day's drama and, once dressed again, she made her way downstairs where she found Vilma in the kitchen with Eve, cooking up an enormous breakfast.

"I am not a cook," their hostess explained, "but I do keep a well-stocked fridge. Eve wanted to be busy so we are accommodating all the food preferences we can think of. Some of it is in the warming oven. Help yourself, Hilary. I don't think Mavis is awake yet but the aroma of good food should do the trick soon enough."

Eve turned toward Hilary and she saw the younger woman looked more or less as normal. Perhaps she was used to dealing with traumatic events caused by her husband. Her recovery seemed abnormally fast to Hilary, who was not yet sure she had actually recovered from the shock.

"We decided to stay by the fire together last night. Whenever we woke it was a comfort to know the fire was there and another body was close by. I feel the better of it and I'm sure Mavis will too."

Hilary left the bustling scene of activity and, carrying two cups of coffee on a tray, went to the adjoining family room to see if Mavis was awake.

Mavis smiled at her approach. She still looked groggy but accepted the steaming coffee with alacrity, patting the couch beside her to invite her friend to sit. Hilary did as indicated and they sipped together in companionable silence for a minute or two.

"How are you feeling?"

"Not bad, considering. The headache is better now but the doctor warned me to take it easy for a day or two."

"Are you up to telling me what happened? I know only the bare outline."

Mavis had been thinking of what she would say to Hilary. There seemed to be no point in hiding the truth and there was a chance it would help to get it out in the open.

"I came home with the shopping from the market. Goodness! All that stuff must still be in the back of the car, Hilary!"

"Don't give that a thought. Just tell me."

"Well, I had the sense of trouble as soon as Eve didn't come to meet me. I tried to phone for help but he was on me before I realized."

She stopped and swallowed more coffee.

Hilary could see this was not going to be easy for her. "Your call to Derek Price saved your lives, Mavis. You did the right thing."

"I don't really remember much of the next bit until I saw Eve in the bedroom tied up. The shock hit me then and I just collapsed. He had to pick me up and throw me onto the other bed. I knew I had to do something quickly or we were both doomed. Eve gave me the idea and I acted on impulse with strength from somewhere I can't begin to guess at.

I wish I had killed him."

This statement chilled Hilary. Her friend Mavis had never sounded so stern. What damage had been done to her? She maintained a calm exterior and spoke from her heart.

"You did enough to make him immobile and that is what counts. You both got out of there."

"Yes. Eve told the police he had sworn to kill her for leaving him. They found him still dazed and lying in the mess of blood and broken glass. He must have been drunk. He was certainly crazy."

"My dear brave Mavis, it's over now. Neither of you will ever have to see him again."

"Oh yes, we will! There's bound to be a court case of some kind."

"As for that, I met a wonderful lawyer today who will get us the best possible representation to save you from repeated trauma. Don't worry about it."

Silence fell. They could hear something being said in the kitchen. It sounded like Vilma had almost burned her hands on a hot dish.

"There is one thing that still bothers me, Hilary. How did he get into the house? I remember unlocking the door when I arrived."

"Eve may have the answer to that question. Let's go and fill a plate with some of the banquet these ladies have prepared for us. We can ask her after we have eaten here by the fire. I've seen a coffee table like this one of Vilma's. The centre cantilevers up to the height of a regular table in a second."

It was a good idea. Sharing food is a time-honoured way to establish normality. Vilma lightened the atmosphere by reciting her errors in the kitchen.

"Eve knows so much! I haven't used half of the appliances in there. Nolan loved to eat out. When we entertained I had a catering company come and cook here for me. Everyone presumed it was all my work and I chose never to disabuse them of that illusion. I learned a lot watching Eve just now."

"So, Vilma, we can take your name off the meals rota at Harmony House?"

"Definitely! I can load the dishwasher or set the table nicely, but you don't want my amateur cooking efforts, Hilary."

Four voices laughed with varying degrees of conviction.

Eve thought Vilma was better than she claimed she was.

Mavis's mind jumped ahead to a future happy day when they were all safe in the kitchen at Harmony House.

Hilary decided Vilma Smith was one of the most generous and accomplished women she had ever met; a woman who was already an invaluable asset to their group.

Later, Vilma took Mavis upstairs for a hot bath and a nap. Hilary and Eve tackled the dishes in the kitchen and Hilary finally got up the nerve to ask Mavis's question about the break-in.

Eve dried her hands on a paper towel and became more solemn than she had been all morning.

"I've been thinking about this, Hilary. All I know is he got inside and found me. I was sorting through the bookcase in the bedroom. You had asked me to pick out the oldest, worn books and save anything I wanted to read. I had my back to the door. I had a split second of warning. I smelled him behind me but it was too late to do anything."

"Don't upset yourself, Eve. You reacted to save Mavis *and* yourself. You should be proud of your actions. The police will find out how he entered. We know it was not through the front door. The security cameras will show his movements. He will never be allowed to bother you again. He is a cowardly criminal. You will be safe with us and he will never find you."

"Thank you, Hilary. I know I have caused a lot of grief for you. I would not have blamed you and Mavis for throwing me out right at the beginning. I would probably be dead by now."

"Don't think about it, Eve. You were meant to find us. We are your family now."

Eve wiped her tears with the remains of the paper towel.

"Well, I came to you with nothing. I will work for years to justify your faith in me. Whatever Harmony House needs, you can call on me."

"The occasional breakfast spread such as the one we just cleaned up will be sufficient payment, Eve Barton. By the way, I think we should use your maiden name from now on."

"Please! This is a new beginning. It deserves a new name."

∽

It was two more days before the women were ready to return to Camden Corners. The broken rear window where Dobrinski had entered, with the help of a folding step stool he had carried to the house in a plastic carrier bag, had first to be repaired. The security system camera had shown his movements and the recording device was removed as evidence. Hilary insisted the camera's recorder was replaced before she would enter the house again.

In the intervening days, Eve, Mavis and Hilary were treated to new clothes from Vilma's extensive wardrobe. Their hostess refused to allow the two who had been attacked to ever see their bedraggled outfits again. She gave them free rein of her walk-in closets and insisted they could choose anything at all as she knew she had to pare down her belongings for Harmony House.

Hilary was the most reluctant to accept this generous offer but even she was seduced by the range of colours and styles in the room set aside for outdoor and indoor clothing, shoes and accessories.

"This is like a magic cave, Vilma!" Eve's eyes were like saucers as she fingered the fabrics and walked along the rows where clothing was arranged in separate colour blocks.

Mavis was speechless.

"Look! I'm not going to stand around here watching. Get on with it. I will send you all back again if you dare emerge without new clothing from the skin outward. The underwear is in that set of drawers on the left. I buy all sizes as the manufacturers vary so much. There are enough mirrors for all of you to see how you look. Have fun!"

It was several minutes before Mavis dared to take down a smart navy suit with matching polka dotted blouse and shoes. She did not expect all the items to fit her but she soon discovered Vilma bought clothing with stretch built in and what looked small on the hanger actually could accommodate a larger frame. The shoes were too small but Mavis would be happy to walk in her running shoes if she could enjoy an outfit of this quality.

Hilary headed to the underwear section. She imagined good-fitting bras and panties would be the required underpinnings. She was astonished to find an entire range of the Spanx she previously saw only on television adverts. She went behind a screen and tried on a set that was difficult to pull over her thighs but it went right up to her chest and gave her an enviable figure.

So this is how women manage to look so fashionable in their middle age!

Since she was taller than Vilma, Hilary expected nothing would be long enough for her frame. She disliked short skirts and bypassed all the suits, trying instead the selection of pants that ranged from high-waisted jeans to smart hip-hugger styles. She soon discovered the drop-waists gave much more length to the pant legs and she chose two casual pairs in dark colours.

Now she had to find tops. Once again she presumed tailored jackets would not fit so she looked further and found drawers full of sweaters and knitted cardigans. She thought Vilma must like to be wrapped in her knitwear for comfort as most of these were generous in proportions.

Happily clad in her new outfit, she turned her attention to Mavis and Eve.

Mavis was trying on a short coat to match the

navy suit. The coat had a detachable hood and a scarf was tucked into one pocket with gloves in the other.

"Have you ever seen anyone so organized!" she exclaimed. "This set-up would save hours of time looking for accessories. I appoint Vilma Smith, Wardrobe Mistress for Harmony House."

"Agreed!" echoed Hilary and Eve.

Eve looked like a different woman in her chosen outfit of a feather-patterned wool dress and jacket. She had quickly found shoes to fit and hoped Vilma would share her unwanted footwear with her as they seemed to take exactly the same size. She noticed neither of her friends had shoes on their feet.

"Over here in this tall cupboard are boots of all kinds. You two should try some on. Vilma must buy out whole shoes stores at once."

"Vilma once mentioned she shops a lot at a store called Maria's Models, or a name something like that. It's in a London mall in town. She must be Maria's best clothes customer but I have to agree with Eve about the shoes. I've never seen such a display."

Hilary added that Jannice said Vilma was also a patron of online shopping, particularly knitwear from an international company called A Plus, which she believed originated in London.

"She does try to support local suppliers, which is a point in her favour."

Mavis chipped in on Vilma's side. "You must admit she takes good care of her things. Some of this vast collection could be years old. It's not all bought at once. If you know how to choose well, clothes and shoes can last for way more than one season."

It took several more minutes but the time passed swiftly as they helped each other to complete the mission of head-to-toe new clothing. Hilary found a lined raincoat and Eve loved the look of a camelhair wrap coat to perfectly complement her dress.

They paraded down the central stairs to show off to Vilma who especially admired the boots.

"That's more like it!" she said triumphantly. "New clothes. New feelings. New beginnings!"

Despite this optimism, Hilary knew the return to Camden Corners would be difficult for Mavis and Eve.

She would have asked Vilma to keep Eve for a few more days but Vilma was heavily involved in Jannice's house. It was necessary to provide company for Eve in case bad memories overcame her.

Hilary decided neither woman would return to

the room where all the fearsome events occurred. Her own bedroom had a queen bed and a comfy couch. She would offer these to Mavis and Eve and sleep downstairs in the living room. The Lazy-Boy chair could extend to a good length. She had often dozed in it when she was living on her own.

Mavis objected strongly to this plan.

"I refuse to turf you out of your bed in your own house, Hilary! I will sleep downstairs. I don't mind in the least. Your long legs need the extra space. After all, it won't be for too much time now that this house is officially for sale."

CHAPTER 21

There was a great deal of detail to coordinate before the six women could take over Harmony House.

It was fortunate that this level of necessary activity distracted them from the events that took place at Camden Corners. At the next group meeting, Hilary downplayed the drama but all were aware of the impact it had on three of their members as the local newspapers had briefly reported the break-in with the news that the culprit had been apprehended and remanded in custody.

Hilary moved swiftly along to the rest of the agenda which was quite absorbing enough to divert everyone's attention.

First there was the news that Harmony House

was theirs and the first installment of the payment had been made.

Second was the closing date of the Camden Corners house.

Third was the engineer's report. The foundations and electrical work of Harmony House were declared excellent and the area for the elevator shaft approved. Once this work was completed they could all begin to move in.

There were cheers around the room.

"Before then, however, we need to do several important things. We need to sort out the decoration issues. We need to assign purpose to the rooms and we must decide on which bedrooms suit which of us best. I have to say, I have arbitrarily appointed the lower level to Honor. She has been kind enough to say this decision can be altered once she is back to full mobility."

"Thank you, Hilary. I want to add, it is not an exclusive area. Any of you can come and go there as you wish. I will have a private bedroom but access to the garden is available any time at all. I am so excited about this opportunity. Oh, and if anybody needs help with finances or internet access, please come to me at once."

Honor's enthusiasm lifted the tone of the meeting and a date on which to gather at the new house was discussed.

As previously arranged, Hilary then gave the floor to Vilma who had offered to help with furniture issues. She smiled over toward Jannice before she began.

"Jannice and I have recently had a crash course on the value, or otherwise, of old furniture and household items. We are taking something incredible to the London Museum's Antiques Fair in a week or so. Jannice and I will fill you all in on that later.

What we discovered was that mid-century teak furniture, similar to what Hilary owns, is having a moment of resurgence but most older, heavier stuff is pretty much worthless unless you can find an older building, such as a church, with the space for large items in good condition. I can't provide furnishings as my house is being sold as is, other than for my own private possessions like clothes, jewellery and a few ornaments. I will buy new bedroom items.

Hilary has kindly offered Eve her choice of furniture from here, and Mavis has selected some of her own fine antique pieces, currently in storage, for Harmony House. I think it will be interesting to see how each bedroom reflects the style of its owner. That applies also to the decoration each of us chooses for our private rooms. If you need help, I am happy to do it. For example, I believe it would be special for any of us who has a set of good china, to choose one place setting for formal meals. We can use ordinary dishes for the rest of the time.

Jannice and I decided to donate most of what remains in her home to the groups who provide furniture for refugees from Syria who are being assisted to get set up here in London. Any extra kitchen wares can be donated in this way after the storage cupboards at Harmony are filled with whatever you all need for cooking your favourite meals.

Something else we are considering is to invite Interior Design students from Fanshawe College to stage Jannice's home for buyers. We hope to get a sale more quickly that way. It could be an idea to request these students come to Harmony House also. There are certainly a few design issues to sort out there!"

No one could disagree with this statement. Hilary then took over the meeting again.

"Vilma, you are so knowledgeable and helpful. Thank you for this summary. I think it's safe to say we are well on our way with two houses sold, one to sell, one house to be handed over to an agent, and one apartment to be vacated. Now, let's fix a date for our next inspection. It will be our first since we became the official owners. I guarantee everything will look different seen from that perspective."

~

The wedding photographer arrived in a van. He brought his assistant, a bright young girl on a Visual Arts work experience placement from Western University. Vilma was not initially impressed by the girl's appearance, especially the silver ring clipped to her eyebrow, but she soon learned how competent Rihanna was with materials and lighting equipment.

It was a mutual decision to take photographs in the hallway of Jannice's home as the bannisters were the original polished oak and the wallpaper was faded almost to oblivion and therefore not in competition with the clothing.

Vilma could not help but think of the first moment she saw Jannice floating down the stairs in what they now called 'The Wedding Dress'. Once Jannice was fastened into the dress properly and had her hair piled on her head under the magnificent hat with just two black, shiny curls cascading to the shoulders, she looked exquisite. Almost as if the dress was made for her. Rihanna and Josh were struck dumb for a moment.

He went back out to his van and brought in more

side lights and a mesh cover for the main light, saying the more diffused lighting would suit the subject better.

Vilma was not present for the actual shooting. She was busy setting out the next outfits which were arranged over the beds in the bedroom at the top of the stairs and where she could hear what was going on below. She and Jannice had selected a stunning slate-blue day dress with a long-sleeved top puffing out a little at the shoulders, and with a peplum waist over a full skirt. The blue fabric was decorated with braid on the high neckline, the cuffs, and in two places around the skirt hem. Under the dust cloth which had covered this outfit, they found a smart blue hat with a long feather attached to the crown and sweeping downward to the back of the neck. It completed the picture perfectly.

Josh placed Jannice with her hand on the front door with the stained glass panel above. It was as if she was going out on the town for afternoon tea with lady friends.

Next came a stunning evening dress in a lilac shade. Vilma powdered Jannice's chest and neck to show off the low neckline and the thin ruffled straps that sat above her shoulder bones. The ruffles were repeated on inset panels all around the skirt. These panels began at the tiny waistline and billowed out to the floor in an inverted V shape. The waist was so small that Vilma knew the woman for whom this dress was intended had to have worn a laced corset. She was surprised when the dress fit Jannice although she claimed to have held her breath the entire time Rihanna was arranging the folds to show off the ruffles and she had to breathe shallowly the rest of the time in case the delicate fabric would tear apart.

Josh had a tall candlestick in his van that looked exactly right for this photograph and Rihanna looped Jannice's hair up, leaving strands around her face and adding long crystal earrings that looked like diamonds in the subtle lighting.

By the time two more photographs were made, both Jannice and her dresser were almost exhausted, but Rihanna, who had helped Jannice to climb back up the stairs and then seen the garments displayed on the bed, begged for just one more. She had picked out the pale gold dress that Vilma was not sure about, as it was neither a low-cut evening dress or a fabric, or colour, likely to be worn during the day. Rihanna loved the monochrome effect of head-to-toe gold and said it would photograph well. Jannice climbed into it and descended the stairs one more time holding a feathered fan of Josh's in her hand.

When they were finished, Josh and Rihanna

joined the women in the kitchen for a cup of tea and ginger biscuits. The inevitable questions began.

"So where did these outfits come from?"

"They came from the back of my attic, in a locked wardrobe, and as far as I know they have been there since I was born."

"Hmmm…. more than likely, much longer than that," said Josh. "I know clothing styles and these are probably late Victorian or possibly Edwardian, which makes them older than this row of houses. The question is, how did they get there?"

Vilma and Jannice exchanged glances. They did have another discovery which they were saving for the Antiques Show but Josh seemed to be knowledgeable about the era and perhaps he could help them.

"I'll get it," confirmed Jannice, as she jumped up and ran upstairs to her bedroom.

Josh and Rihanna contented themselves with more cookies and waited to see what was coming.

She arrived with a letter in her hand and placed it carefully in the centre of the kitchen table facing toward Rihanna and Josh.

Dear Ma,

I know this is going to be hard for you to believe but you know the circumstances.

My mistress has been quite ill since the dreadful ferry capsized on the river and her beloved

Sidney was drownded. At one time we thought she would pass away from grief as she were

proper pale and sickly and the Doctor had me bring her sweet milk every two hours on the dot.

Now, she is a little improved, thanks be to The Good Lord, but she does not want to

see ever again the beautiful clothes specially made for her wedding day. She swore to me she will never marry another man after Sidney. She gave me the job of removing the lot from the house before she rises from her bed again.

Ma, I cannot bear to throw these lovely things away or even sell them. I will always see

the picture in my mind of my Miss Amelia standing before the long glass admiring herself and telling me about her honeymoon plans in Europe.

Can you find a place in our old home for these dresses? I know you have Bridget, Maeve and Ryan and little Maisie to care for but I will send a man from the big house to help stow them for you if you can see your way to storing them until I can think what to do next.

Please Ma. Send a note back with the messenger boy to let me know what you decide.

I am praying for guidance in this. I am enclosing this week's wages as usual.

Your loving daughter,
Erin O'Connor.

"Well, now, this is quite amazing. Did you find it with the clothes?"

"It was in an envelope pinned to the very back of the wardrobe. We only found it recently and we are not sure what to do with it."

"This is historical information," said Rihanna. "It needs to go to the university, along with the clothing.

I am pretty sure the incident Erin refers to is the 1881 capsizing of the Victoria Ferry in Springbank Park. They used to run regular ferry boats from the Forks of the Thames up the river to the park. When this disaster happened there were almost two hundred passengers drowned, mostly women and children wearing the long, heavy clothing of the time. You can still see the plaque erected on the path by the place where it happened."

Vilma recovered first from the vision of so many women and children struggling in the river to keep their heads above water amidst a nightmare scene of screaming and shouting.

"The problem for us, Rihanna, is that we need to raise money with these outfits. We can't just donate them."

"No problem there, Jannice."

Josh was re-reading the letter and thinking fast. "You have a great story here. I have a pal at the newspaper who would love access to these photos and the story of the desolated bride. I noticed her name, Amelia. It's a long shot, and I would need to get Eldon House on board with this, but there's an outside chance the Amelia in the letter is the favourite granddaughter of Amelia Harris, the matriarch of the family. Her nickname was Milly and I think she never married.

Whatever, the publicity would bump up the price of these artifacts and the person who bought them could gift them to the Historical Society, or the Museum, or Eldon House, or the University when they wished to. You would get the money you need first of all."

Vilma's mind was buzzing.

"That's an absolutely brilliant idea, Josh. What do you think, Jannice?'

"I can't believe all this. It's a lot to take in when you put the parts together. Let me get it straight.

So Erin gave the clothes to her mother, am I right?"

Heads nodded around the table.

"But this house can't be the one the clothes arrived at because it likely wasn't built then and it was never big enough for a family the size of the one Erin describes. I am coming back to the question of how the wardrobe got here and why I knew nothing about it from my parents?"

Jannice was right. There were still questions to be answered.

Josh was the first to respond.

"You may never have all the answers, but I can speculate a little. Your family name is Irish, right?

Lots of families immigrated to Canada in the Irish famines and took up work labouring or in service.

It's possible, I suppose, that your ancestors lived in London, or even Lucan, where there was a big community of famous Irish families, including the Donnellys. They were used to crowding into small cottages at that time. Four or five in a bed wasn't uncommon."

Rihanna interrupted her employer. "I think it's likely Erin's salary was keeping her family's head above water. As the children grew up and took on jobs, the housing situation would improve and a better home could be found.

I believe the wardrobe moved along with the

family. If you think about it, there might have been accusations of stealing if the contents of that wardrobe had been revealed. No poor immigrant family could afford clothes like these we saw today. Over time it might have become one of those family secrets, locked away and mostly forgotten."

Jannice had a strange look on her face as she listened to Rihanna's theories.

"Do you know, I think you have hit the nail on the head, so to speak. I remember now, when I was a wee girl my papa spoke about his mother being 'in service' once upon a time. I thought it was *a place* he spoke about. The term meant nothing to me then. I never heard another word about 'service' as work until today. It all begins to make sense."

"Well, if you approve, I will send you proofs of today's photographs and you can tell me if you want to go ahead with an article in the newspaper. I think it would be best published before the antiques event at the museum for maximum impact."

Jannice still looked bemused by all she had heard. Vilma responded in her place.

"Josh and Rihanna, it's been quite an experience with you today. I think I can speak for Jannice and ask you to go ahead. If your reporter friend is willing, send him along here. I know he will get an interesting story for the paper. And thank you both for everything."

Later that day, the letter was carefully taken upstairs and stowed, with its original envelope, in a folder Vilma had found.

The dresses were returned to the wardrobe inside their cotton covers and the wardrobe locked up tight.

The ladder to the attic was left down since traffic up and down had been so frequent. Jannice decided she would do some more dusting and cleaning up there in case the reporter wanted more photos.

They went back to the kitchen, and more cups of tea, so they could talk over everything that had been said there. The story of Erin O'Connor's life was amazing to them. Whether or not the trousseau belonged to a member of the Harris family was not as important to them as the tiny insight into life in the past when London was a much smaller town.

Vilma asked Jannice if she would come with her to tour Eldon House.

"I confess I have never been there, but now I have a real urge to see what life was like for a rich family in those days, especially if there is information about how the servants lived."

"I think we should go together as soon as this place is sold. If Josh is right and the story helps us get a good price, it would be a fitting tribute to a young Irish girl who must have been a trusted servant to her mistress."

They shook hands on that decision and went back to the mundane business of clearing and cleaning but their hearts were lighter with the hopes that had been given to them.

CHAPTER 22

W hen the six women converged on the Harmony House site, they found it was a hive of activity.

Hilary tracked down the site supervisor while the rest of the party had to be content with admiring the building from the safety of the garages to the side of the property.

Once Hilary had been equipped with a hard hat, she was permitted to enter and speak to the man with the name Frank Watson written on his yellow hat.

"I was under the impression the major work had been finished, Mr. Watson."

"We are still working on the elevator shaft. The stairs have been removed, but the problems arose with the secondary section of the shaft from the kitchen area down to the basement level. A new opening has to be made to accommodate the elevator. We are examining the possibilities of using two or more kitchen cupboards for this."

"I see. Will the laundry area be affected?"

"I hope not. If we have to move it, there's sufficient space down there but plumbing and electrics may have to be reset and that takes time."

"Mr. Watson, the future residents of this home are here with me. Is it possible for us to enter by the rear and inspect only the west side of the building, keeping well away from your workers?"

He rubbed a calloused hand over his face as he considered this request.

"I hate to turn you away. Is it Mrs. Dempster?"

She confirmed his assumption with a nod.

"Could you wait for about 30 minutes? We have a lunch break then. I'll get the boys to set up a tape beyond where you should not enter for safety reasons, then you can do whatever you need to for the next hour. Will that suit?"

"Perfectly! Thank you."

The women were quite pleased with this solution and spent the time wandering around the property. Spring-like weather had made an appearance lately but it was more than likely to vanish again soon.

They viewed the tower-side of the building and speculated how much storage they would get from the three double garages, then they walked around to the rear gardens, where the flowerbeds were now visible and the first shoots of bulbs were pushing up toward the light.

"This is going to be a wonderful outdoor area," exclaimed Mavis. "I have never had a garden of this size. It will be super to work here and keep what has been done in the best of shape. Is anyone else interested in gardening?"

Hilary, who had walked off to the back of the garden, waved her hand in assent but the others were too busy looking through the windows into the lower house area with Honor, who was explaining the layout for them.

Mavis was about to follow Hilary when she caught sight of a woman approaching from the street. She was not wearing a coat and Mavis guessed she must be a neighbour.

"Hello, there! Can I help you?"

"Possibly. I came over from the house next door to see if you were the new owners."

"We are, but we have not yet moved in. I am Mavis Montgomery."

"Good. Louise Ridley. My husband Dennis and I live next door. I hope you don't think it's a typical nosy neighbour enquiry but we have been wondering what on earth is going on here. You see we have been watching the house being built for some time now, and then no one moved in after the builders left. Quite frankly, we are confused. Our house value could be affected if something strange is going on here."

"I see." Mavis was not sure how to respond to this enquiry but she could see genuine worry on Louise Ridley's face. This would be their nearest neighbour and it was important to start off in the right way and establish a good relationship.

"I'm not sure if you will think it strange, Louise, but we are a group of six London women who have decided to live together in support of each other. We are all ordinary people and we will welcome your help in this process. At the moment we are waiting for an elevator to be installed. After that we will move in. Have you ever been inside?"

"No. There's never been anyone in residence who could be asked. I am relieved to hear you are not some weird commune or wiccan group. The woman who came here once with a little girl had such a fight on the front porch with, I presume, her husband, that the whole neighbourhood heard them. I am glad *she* will not be back. The sale sign went up shortly after that incident and since then, nothing."

"Well, you and your husband will be our first guests. It's a remarkable large house, Louise, with ample space for all of us. I hope we will be friends. It's always good to know someone who can tell us about the neighbourhood facilities. Sorry, to leave you, but I can see the construction supervisor signalling to me. I have to round everyone up. I am glad we met."

"Not nearly as glad as I am. I will be telling Dennis what you said as soon as he gets home this evening.

My goodness, it's still a chilly wind, isn't it! I must run. Bye for now."

Mavis watched as Louise disappeared through a gap in the hedge separating the two properties. She could not see more than the tip of a chimney of the Ridley home as the line of tall spruce trees shielded it from view.

Her assessment of the conversation was that Louise and Dennis were concerned owners who feared their property would be de-valued by anything untoward next door. It would be her job to reassure them and she was confident the first steps had been taken.

The partial house inspection revealed several

changes. Furniture had been removed from the main floor and the spaces could now be seen clearly. The first discussion was about who would occupy the lower tower room and Vilma suggested that both tower bedrooms should be the domain of Hilary and Mavis.

"After all, you two are responsible for this entire project. You should have the prime spots. Does everyone agree?"

To the dismay of Mavis and Hilary, this was a unanimous decision. Neither woman would have claimed these special rooms for themselves but it would be churlish to refuse the generosity of the others.

Hilary immediately reminded them Harmony House was to be owned jointly and all decisions would be voted on. "I want you to know that our first room designations may be temporary until we see what is needed most."

"I want to underline that," spoke up Honor. "It's the same agreement as I accepted when Hilary suggested the lower level for me. We can't know yet how we will settle in here. Let's not be too possessive at first. Everything could change in a few months."

"Exactly! I am going to schedule a meeting for

two months from our moving in and we will reassess things then. All in agreement?"

"Yes!" was the resounding response.

Another good sign, thought Mavis.

What wonderful women, thought Eve.

I want to see the two other major rooms, thought Jannice. She followed Vilma who headed straight for the dining room. She had an idea.

"What do you think of making this room our general living room? We could leave the dark panelling. It would be mainly a winter gathering place as we would be outdoors in the warmer weather. There's a handsome fireplace here and we could put comfy chairs around. A piano would be a nice touch and we could have one of those televisions installed above the fireplace behind a screen made from a painting.

I am glad those other awful paintings have been removed."

"Won't we need a dining room, once in a while?" Hilary had heard Vilma's voice and had listened to her plan. Eve spoke up next.

"I've been thinking about that very thing, Hilary. I believe the lovely airy space in the kitchen is perfect for a casual dining table big enough for all of us. The French doors lead out to the small deck from there and it's much handier to the kitchen."

"Eve, you have already appointed yourself as Kitchen Supervisor and I think that's a sensible idea. Vilma is right. This is a grand winter common room where we can enjoy the view across the front yard. The panelling won't bother us. It will be a cozy effect in the evenings with the fire burning.

Now what about the room on the other side of the hall with that white carpet?"

The group turned around and walked back to the left of the entrance, passing the vivid violet stair carpet on the way, with a shudder.

Honor hoped the workmen would spill something on it and ruin the whole thing. It was going to be expensive to replace.

Hilary stood back and allowed the others to enter and walk around. She liked the way in which the group recognized the strengths of each person and gave everyone's opinion equal weight. She knew another good idea would emerge before long.

"I think we could save money on replacing this carpet if we designated this room for occasional use only."

"Do you mean something like a quiet room?"

"Right! It's a corner room so it could be our Corner Contemplation spot. No drinks or television and no phones, just books or magazines or letter writing."

"In a Jane Austen style with a writing desk?"

"Absolutely, Hilary!"

"Well, to be practical," said Jannice. "We will still need rugs to cover some of the carpet and I don't see why this could not be our guest room also. A pull-out bed couch could be here for occasional guests and the powder room is right next door in the entrance hall. We could easily enlarge the washroom by taking a section from that huge coat closet for a shower."

Vilma clapped her hands together and everyone laughed and congratulated Jannice.

"I think Vilma's good design ideas are washing off on me!" she declared.

After this joint planning meeting, the decision about which bedroom belonged to which person was settled very quickly. The four rooms off the upper balcony were the exact same size and each had an ensuite washroom and a stunning view over the back garden. Two of the washrooms had a bath instead of a shower and that made the decision easier.

Eve chose the one nearest the elevator so she could quickly go down to the kitchen. Jannice and Vilma picked the next two in line leaving the one beside the tower room free for Honor if she should feel she wanted to be closer to the others when her hip was better.

There was no more time to check things out, as the crew arrived back with their supervisor.

"How did it go, ladies?" Frank Watson was pleased to see no one had passed through his safety barrier.

"We did everything we needed to. All we need now is for the elevator to be completed so we can finally move into our new home."

"That's what we're here for, Mrs. Dempster. And if you wouldn't mind, we want to get on with it."

CHAPTER 23

Hilary Dempster could not wait to move out of Camden Corners. Every night spent with Eve on the sofa was a reminder of the risk they had taken and what almost happened because they had once left Eve on her own in this house.

She had employed a company to come to the house and strip out the carpet in the second bedroom. They then sanded the floor boards and painted on a triple coating of varnish which brought up the wood grain nicely. To the new floor she added two rugs from other parts of the house. After the beds were replaced, and the remaining picture on the wall removed, she locked the door again. She had no intention of allowing anyone to enter there.

In the meantime, she went around the house

placing green stickers on the furniture that was needed for Harmony House. With Eve's help she did the same in the kitchen. Last of all, she invited the new owners to return and select anything remaining that they would like to keep in the house and she gave them a very good price, thereby ensuring there was almost nothing left to dispose of when the three women finally departed from number 46.

She observed that Mavis and Eve were no less anxious than she to move on. They often sat together in the daytime or when watching television in the evening. Mavis made a point of closing the heavy drapes after quickly scanning the back yard. The home invasion and its consequences were weighing on her mind. Eve was seemingly the least affected. She took courage from the assurances of the police that her husband was not to be released before his trial. Hilary had to believe this situation was in fact preferable to the daily fear of Howard's uncertain temperament. It made her wonder what kind of hell Eve Barton had lived in for years.

One Sunday night when Mavis and Eve were watching 60 Minutes, Hilary went up to her office to check over some figures. It was a tricky business to coordinate the dates for vacating her house and arranging for a removal van to have access to Harmony as well as releasing Mavis's furniture from storage. She was hoping to employ one removal van to do both jobs on the same day. Vilma was working on some publicity scheme for Jannice's place but she had not yet revealed what that was about. If all went well, Vilma would supervise the sale of the O'Connor home.

Thank God for Vilma! She's a free agent and has donated her time to help others. What would we have done without her?

Hilary was just circling dates on her calendar when the phone rang on her desk.

Who would be calling on a Sunday night?

"Mother! Is that you?"

"Desmond! What's wrong?"

"Why should something be wrong, mother?"

"I'm sorry. It's just that you don't call very often and I was surprised."

"Well, as it happens, *I was surprised* recently and that's why I'm calling you. A school pal from Camden Corners came to see me in Toronto and in the course of conversation about this and that, he mentioned the old place was up for sale."

"Yes, that's right, Desmond. A couple from Mississauga has bought the house. They will be moving in quite soon."

"When were you going to tell me this?"

His belligerent tone was beginning to annoy Hilary. She sat up straighter ready to do battle if necessary. She had no illusions about her son. He was, unfortunately, a mercenary character. Since moving to the big city for work, he was chronically short of money. She subsidized his lifestyle ever since his father's death but if he was expecting an early inheritance he was going to be out of luck.

"This all happened quite fast, Desmond. I saw an opportunity to establish a place for my old age together with friends who would look after me, and I them. You know I have never had any great liking for Toronto, even if you ever offered to take me in. Similarly, it seems unlikely you would want to move back here to London and care for me in my old age."

"Good God, mother! You are not that old. All those concerns are far in the future, I would think. Why are you making such decisions right now? Has something happened? A fall? A medical emergency? What?"

"I am quite well at the moment, thank you for asking, son. The truth is, I am a woman alone and that can be frightening. I felt I needed to plan for my future while I still had an asset."

There was a momentary silence. She knew he was calculating something.

"So, what did the place sell for?"

She named a figure that was several thousand dollars below the actual selling price, and waited for his reaction.

"Not bad for London. Not bad at all. You should be able to pass on a third of that without any trouble."

She knew at once what he meant and her heart fell. Each time they spoke she hoped a change of mindset would come with maturity. But not yet, it seems.

"That will not happen, Desmond. You must understand this house is mine. Your father's will makes that very clear. Any benefit to you, will come from my will, which, as you say, is some time in the future, God Willing. I need all of this money to guarantee my place in a larger home on the outskirts of the city."

"But that's ridiculous, Mom."

Here it comes.

"You know how tight things are for me. I didn't get that promotion I was counting on. How will I afford to come and see you without the old house to stay in? Is that what you want? Complete isolation from your only flesh and blood?"

She tried to calm her shaking limbs. There was

no point in prolonging this agony. It would end in acrimony as always.

"Don't worry about that, Desmond. There will be a guest suite for the convenience of friends and family. Let me know when you wish to see me and I will reserve it for you.

Now I need to go. Take care, my dear.

Goodbye."

She placed the handset down slowly and carefully but not before she heard the shattering sound of his anger at his end of the line.

It's over. He knows now. I can move ahead with my plans without dreading this conversation. I doubt I will see him in London again.

She dabbed at her eyes and breathed out and in without allowing any other thoughts to enter her mind.

Downstairs she heard the door open and Mavis's voice call for her. It was time for their nightcap; tea and talk about the day ahead.

"I'll be right there, Mavis. Wait for me."

Although most of the coordination was now occurring by telephone for the sake of speed, Vilma and Jannice had a reason to call for another meeting of the co-housing group. They felt it was time to share their good news and they wanted to do it in style.

Vilma contacted Hilary with the invitation to her North London house and Jannice called Honor, assuring her they would share a cab ride to Vilma's. The purpose of this meeting was kept under wraps. The excuse was the final chance to gather at Vilma's since the house was soon to be transferred to her step-children's lawyer.

There was a bit of grumbling at Hilary's.

"We have so much to do, Mavis. I can't imagine why Vilma wants to be bothered with this meeting."

"I'm sure she has her reasons and we can't refuse after all she did for us not long ago."

Hilary noticed how reluctant her friend was to mention the awful business of Dobrinski's attack. She suspected Mavis was not sleeping well. At first she blamed the Lazy-Boy chair in which she had chosen to sleep, but as Mavis looked more and more drawn around the face, she concluded that it was her mind's discomfort causing the symptoms, rather than her body's. Once more Hilary longed for the move to Harmony to be closer to completion.

In the end, they were all glad to get out of Camden Corners for an evening of what Vilma had eventually announced as 'a celebration'. Eve had a secret hope of getting another chance to raid the closets. The more she admired the dress and jacket outfit she had acquired there, the more she realized how dowdy her old clothes were. She decided to wear the new dress in the hopes it might prompt Vilma to offer more. She would never dare to ask.

Mavis just wanted to get away from her memories for a few hours. She had never before been subjected to bodily violence and it weighed on her mind how helpless she felt in the face of Howard Dobrinski's malice and physical strength. The fact of her own need to resort to violence against him was hidden away at the back of her mind. She knew she was not yet strong enough to deal with that troubling aspect. She hid all of this from her house partners in fear that Eve would feel obliged to revisit the episode. Of all of them, Eve appeared to be recovering the best but then, Mavis decided, she was finally relieved of the daily worry she must have endured while living with that beast of a man.

The trio arrived at Vilma's house in good spirits. They found Jannice and Honor already started on cocktails and a veritable feast of appetizers displayed in the kitchen and attended by a uniformed young man and woman from a catering company. The house was redolent with delicious aromas and both

Vilma and Jannice were positively bouncing with excitement.

"Welcome! Welcome! Dinner will be served later. Please fill your plates and glasses and follow me to the dining room where all will be revealed."

Vilma was not joking. Displayed on large posters all around the walls were the photographs of Jannice in the beautiful antique clothing from the attic wardrobe. Glasses and plates were placed on the table and promptly forgotten as the visitors moved from one to another of the posters and exclaimed at the remarkable effect of petite Jannice's form encased in those amazing dresses, captured in poses reminiscent of a bygone era.

How? What? Where? Why? resounded in a growing crescendo of surprise until Vilma clapped her hands and requested everyone to sit and hear the tale from Jannice's lips. This was accomplished with the aid of the photographs and a copy of the letter passed around from hand to hand.

"This is extraordinary! How did you two conspirators manage to keep this concealed for so long?"

"Well, Hilary, we have been busy setting things up for our next reveal."

"What next?" Eve was quivering with excitement.

Vilma took over and explained about the article soon to appear in the next edition of The Londoner, timed to bring attention to the Museum's Antiques event which had already garnered considerable interest among Londoners.

"We were interviewed for the article, which was quite exciting in itself. There will be photographs, of course, and mention will be made of the fact Jannice's house is for sale."

"Don't forget, Vilma, there will also be a photo of the actual wardrobe in the article!"

Jannice was bubbling over with the chance to finally talk about all this. She had previously been sworn to secrecy by the editor who said nothing should diminish the impact of the article if they wanted to get results.

"You really had no idea this treasure trove was waiting in your attic all these years?"

"Nope. No clue. Thank heaven Vilma made me go up there and look around. If I had sold the house as it was before we started to clear it out, someone else would have discovered all this and a piece of O'Connor family history could have passed me by."

Between bites of appetizers and sips of drinks, many more questions were asked and answered until Vilma had to collect plates and ask her guests to move to the living room until the caterers could set the table and serve the first course of the meal.

Jannice, the star of the show, held court while

this was accomplished and talked to the women about the feel of the hand-made trousseau and how Amelia could have possibly coped with the loss of her fiancé in such a dramatic fashion.

"Well, first on my list of outings will be a walk in Springbank Park to find that historical plaque!" declared Hilary. I must surely have walked past it without noticing. You have brought the disaster to life with your story, Jannice. What an adventure!"

"We will see how it affects the house sale. That's the next objective. The photographer is convinced an antiques dealer will want to buy the clothes collection and the reporter is attending the show to see if he is right."

"I think you will cause quite a stir at Museum London. Have you thought of appearing in one of the outfits? Perhaps the gorgeous blue day dress with the dashing hat?"

"That's a marvellous idea, Mavis. I will do it! Thank you."

The conversation continued throughout the meal's three courses with items of interest related to Harmony House gradually creeping in. Up to now, things were moving ahead as planned. The elevator issues had been solved with the minimum of disruption. Hilary and Mavis had been summoned to the lawyer's office for the transfer of the keys and the signing of papers accompanied by another deposit of 20% of the cost. Following this all the signees would receive their contracts and become official co-owners of Harmony House as soon as the final payment schedule had been approved.

Vilma produced a bottle of champagne and a tray of crystal glasses for a toast.

Jannice raised her glass convinced for the first time that she would meet and surpass her portion of the sale price.

Vilma teared up at the contrast between these friendly women and Nolan's adult children who continued to disdain her at every attempt at reconciliation.

Eve rejoiced that the main part of her inheritance money would soon be safely deposited in the developer's hands and not ever accessible to her husband.

Mavis thought of her antique furniture soon to be released from storage and installed in her new bedroom where the happy memories of her beloved Peter would accompany them.

Honor looked around the table and blessed the day she had spotted the little advert in the grocery store and recognized an opportunity.

Hilary felt her heart expand with sheer joy at the accomplishment this table of diverse women, soon to be housemates, represented.

It would have been more than enough of a celebration already, but Vilma had one more trick up her sleeve.

"Honor, you missed out on the last closet raid. Please accompany us upstairs where I have now removed all the clothing items I wish to keep. These are in storage for a short time with the rest of my personal possessions. Everything else you see is available to whomever it fits. I have provided large shopping bags so you can remove the contents tonight. Tomorrow I vacate this house and go to a hotel until Harmony House is ready for me. All the remaining clothes and shoes are to be collected and taken to Goodwill, so help yourselves, ladies!"

CHAPTER 24

After weeks of teasing weather with the occasional warm day reversing to bitter winds and overnight frosts, Mother Nature relented. The sun shone in a clear blue sky, the air smelled of growing things and the population of London emerged from the winter stupor and rejoiced in the outdoors again.

Mavis woke after her final night on the Lazy-Boy with a sense of relief. Today they were moving to Harmony House at long last. Her furniture had been rescued from storage and placed in her new tower bedroom where it assumed a stately demeanour matching the exterior of the house. She elected to leave the windows uncovered as the curved base of the tower was sheltered by the wrap-around porch.

A selection of her favourite framed photographs waited to be placed on the walls and there were things to be sorted through, but all these tasks could wait. The day was perfect for outdoor thinking.

She went into Hilary's kitchen and saw the appliances ready in their boxes. The coffee machine was still available and she filled it to the top with cold water and waited while the coffee brewed for the last time in this house she had called home for months. With a steaming hot cup in her hands she stepped outside the front door and breathed the soft moist air. Most of the front of the house was taken up by the double driveway. There was only a passing attempt at a garden consisting of a bush or two surrounded by river stones. The rear area was not much better and had suffered from neglect over the winter not to mention the heavy footprints of police and a pair of window installers.

Mavis had decided never to enter that part of the Camden Corners property and her resolve was maintained.

And yet, today her mind turned to thoughts of the garden at Harmony House. That grand sweep of lawn leading to the house was going to require a decent lawnmower at the very least. She recalled some mention of a gardener and hoped she could track him down through Louise Ridley next door. As for the garden at the back of the property, that was a far different proposition as it had already been divided into plant beds and pathways. Her fingers itched to grasp a trowel and begin to turn over the soil and plant some herbs. In the Ontario Cottage she had a nice kitchen garden and some perennial plants. None of the others had expressed any real interest in garden work but she knew they would appreciate the benefits, especially the women whose bedrooms overlooked the back garden.

Thoughts of the patio and summer weather with leisure to sit and admire a growing garden, brought the realization that one item missing from Hilary's list of Things To Be Done was the purchase of a set of garden furniture. There would need to be sufficient tables and chairs for all the house members. It would be an expensive purchase and the lounge chairs would require good storage over the winter.

On one of their recent expeditions to explore the Harmony facilities they obtained the keys to the set of garages. There were three double garages attached in a row on the west of the property, at the end of the driveway. Hilary was most concerned about the paved path from there to the side entrance to the house. It was not wide enough for a car and meant groceries would have to be conveyed by hand in all weathers, taken up the three steps onto the verandah and then down again into the basement level to reach the elevator. She had decried this arrangement as 'pure lunacy' and gently cursed the developer for short-sightedness, declaring it obvious he did not do the shopping for his family.

Mavis thought it possible to find a trolley of some kind to ferry the groceries to the side entrance. A waterproof covering would keep everything dry and a large golf umbrella would protect the women in bad weather. It would do for the time being.

Now, she began to consider the garages as valuable space for cars and other things. The women had three cars at their disposal but that left one and a half garage spaces free. Perhaps the garden furniture and tools could occupy one of those spaces leaving one entire garage for storage or messy work like crafting. The idea of hobbies was not one that had been pursued yet. As she thought back over the months since the co-housing project was initiated, it was not surprising some things had been missed. She hoped no really vital items were neglected; ones that would cause trouble in the future.

She made a mental note to discuss the garden issues with Hilary as soon as they had settled in.

Today's tasks were enough to be concerned with. Hilary's teak dining room set was gone, together with Eve's chosen items, to Harmony House, but her bedroom furniture and the kitchen wares were being moved in an hour or two. Mavis had packed her car with clothes the night before and she meant to leave Camden Corners behind forever.

She sipped the last of her cooling coffee and went inside to prepare to meet the challenges of this last day. One happy thought crossed her mind. In a week or two she would be able to retrieve her cat from the neighbours who had been caring for her. The odd visit to see Marble had not been enough to fill the gap in her life the little creature had left. Once Marble was installed in the huge tower room with the familiar furniture, Mavis would be content.

From her downtown hotel room at The London Armouries, Vilma had made frequent expeditions to furniture stores to view their bedroom suites. Nothing seemed to meet her requirements until, in despair one night, she researched 'modern bed-sitting-room furnishings' and hit the jackpot. She found exactly what she required and immediately ordered their best quality set, along with a company employee to install the entire system in her new bedroom. After this was done, she placed a sign on the door prohibiting entrance and moved her clothing and other personal items into their places for a future reveal. This left her free to spend more time with Jannice's house sale project.

Downtown to Old East was a mere minute or two and she traversed Dundas Street many times while the fervor over the 'O'Connor History Mystery' as the newspaper titled it, finally ground to a halt.

Josh had been right all along. The delicate clothes and accessories were snapped up by a collector as soon as the first article appeared in the paper. Josh suspected the purchaser was buying on behalf of the London Museum but he could not prove it.

After that, there was competition among the dealers at the Antiques event to be allowed to inspect the wardrobe for further clues and a veri-table parade of historians and the simply curious arrived daily at Jannice's door. Vilma kept watch over this parade while attempting to clear out the last of the old furnishings from the house. As it happened, she was helped in this task by the number of people who 'just wanted a souvenir of the history house' and who departed with a variety of items ranging from stained teacups to dilapidated kitchen chairs.

It was only in the final week before the Harmony House move-in date that she noticed a young couple arriving and spending an hour wandering around without saying much. Jannice was upstairs packing her clothes and frequently interrupted in order to escort the latest curiosity seekers up to the attic.

The couple lingered until the others left, when they approached Vilma and asked if she would close the front door and request the home owner to meet with them.

Vilma fetched Jannice at once and whispered to her that she thought something unusual was about to happen.

The four settled in the kitchen with Vilma and Jannice standing, and the couple occupying the only remaining chairs. The young man looked directly at Jannice as he spoke.

"We are Kathleen and Patrick O'Connor. We read about you in the newspapers and although we do not believe we are actually related to you, Miss O'Connor, we were struck by your story.

Kathleen and I are brother and sister. We are the only members of our family still living in Canada. The rest of the surviving O'Connors are now back in Ireland or living in the United States. I have a good job with IBM in London, in project development, and my sister teaches Kindergarten locally.

We came today because we want to make a private offer on your house. We know the price you are asking for and we feel we can meet that price but by the time you add on the realtor fees on both sides of the deal, we might be unable to succeed in a bidding war."

He stopped to let the impact of his words sink in and his sister took up the tale.

"You see, we were brought up in a house very like this one outside Stratford. Our parents were struck down by an unusual immune disease. They decided to pursue experimental treatment in Mexico as nothing available here in Canada was relieving their symptoms.

A family friend took us in when a contractor discovered asbestos in the Stratford house. The damage was so extensive the house was destroyed and the area quarantined. Our father sued the city for causing their ill health, but by the time a settlement was worked out in the courts, both our parents had passed away."

The silence in the tiny kitchen was palpable.

Jannice thought this couple understood about tragedy and could relate to Amelia's story.

Hilary was jumping ahead calculating Jannice's financial situation and hoping she would not let her compassion for these two youngsters undercut the money she needed for Harmony House.

Patrick resumed the sad story.

"We've been sharing rented accommodation for the last three years and saving every penny for a place of our own near our work. We think this is the place where we would feel at home again."

Jannice gulped and was grateful she had not allowed the experts to 'stage' her home for buyers. Every little thing still remaining in this place would be a precious reminder to these young people. She had already taken what she needed. The rest would be theirs without question.

The decision was quickly made and a handshake sealed the deal.

Vilma said nothing to discourage her friend. She was just grateful that the price given for the antique clothing had been so high. Jannice was financially safe for the time being.

Honor Pace was temporarily disconnected. Her equipment was in boxes laid out and labelled by the door with all the attendant cords and power bars safely stowed away. Her clothes, including the three casual outfits she got from Vilma Smith, were packed in the one case she owned, and a few dishes and ornaments occupied the last box.

There's was nothing left to do, other than wait for the man with the van to arrive.

With no keyboard and no smart phone, (the phone was switched off and zipped inside her carry bag in case it should be lost or damaged during the move), Honor found herself with no defence against the thoughts and memories in her brain. To prevent these from overwhelming her each night, she took two sleeping pills. Most nights that worked to keep the worrying thoughts at bay. But now, at this moment of transition from one period of her life to another, she was vulnerable.

She tried to focus on the spread sheet information. It had successfully shown her goal was met just yesterday when her last month's rent had been returned to her. She was officially a valid partner in the co-housing group. Even this achievement could not still her mind, however.

Felicity sneaked in and took up residence.

What was she doing today? Where was she and how was she? Did she ever spare a passing thought for her twin sister or was she just as determined as ever to blot out her very existence? Coming to London from Vancouver, finding a new job and dying her hair bright red could not disguise the fact staring back at Honor from her mirror. She was only one half of a whole. She had a missing half. No matter what she did or where she hid away, that empty space remained unfilled.

She was about to take a huge risk by moving in with these women. Yes, they were all pleasant and friendly but they thought they knew something about Honor Pace and the truth was, they knew next to nothing about her. She would hide away in the basement office and hope to remain undiscovered, but she knew there would come a time when Felicity would succumb to the same realization of a missing part of her life. She would track her down again and the whole nasty business would start up just as it always did.

The intercom jangled. "You ready Miss Pace? I'll bring the guys up and give you a hand with the elevator."

It was another move in a succession of moves. This one might be different. At least she would have people around her if the worst happened. She had tried to exist on her own but it had not helped.

What was the point of isolating yourself from life? All that created was endless days and nights with no sound of a real human voice.

This move must be an answer. She really needed an answer.

~

Hilary arrived at Harmony House with her car full and her heart light. Mavis was following close behind with Eve. Nothing was going to spoil this day although Mavis's reminder about the lack of outdoor furniture was certainly a downer and cast doubt on the efficiency of Hilary's Notes and Priorities system.

They unloaded, and Eve and Hilary used the elevator to speed the last of their portable possessions upstairs to the bedroom floor. Hilary could not help noticing the continuing eyesore of the purple stair carpet.

A decision had been made to delay the purchase of a new carpet.

"After all," stated Vilma, "the workmen have trailed up and down here for weeks and the delivery men will do the same until everyone is settled. A new carpet might well be ruined before it's paid for. Better to wait and see what is left in the contingency fund."

Hilary felt relieved. Vilma could always be counted on for a dose of common sense. She would try to avert her eyes and focus instead on all the other improvements.

When she finally entered the double doors to the tower bedroom and closed them behind her, she stopped and took the first deep breath of the day.

She was here at last. The germ of an idea that had presented itself to her so many months before, had now blossomed into this magnificent home for six women who would be both friend and support for each other through whatever vicissitudes life might bring. By some magical alchemy, she and Mavis had found these four partners who each would contribute to their joint venture in their own individual ways.

She looked around the spectacular tower room with its windows overlooking the side lawn, the garages, and peeping above the tall spruce stand, the chimneys and roof of the Ridley home next door. With the pink drapes and bed coverings gone and the crystal sconces replaced, the room was less of a princess palace and more of the subdued style Hilary Dempster preferred. She felt a twinge of guilt that she had possession of this prime space with a four-piece washroom and a walk-in closet. It was more than she actually needed, but after weeks of sharing her sleeping quarters with Eve, it was going to be wonderful to have this private space all to herself.

She knew privacy was the key ingredient to make Harmony House fit its optimistic name. Every person needed a place to retire to, where they could be alone. Mark Dempster had taught her that in the early days of their marriage when she was eager to spend every waking, and sleeping, hour within his arms.

"Give me space to breathe, darling. I'll return to you refreshed, I promise."

On one of their holiday trips, they had found a little statue of a hooded monk standing in contemplation of nothing in particular. It had become a silent signal. When it appeared on the dinner table Hilary knew what it signified and she smiled and went off to do something by herself.

It was a bitter pill to swallow if that nasty Josette Delacour had told the truth about Mark's extramarital activity. It cast doubt on some of the time he spent away from her but it might explain why their son had dishonest tendencies. She shuddered at these thoughts. She must be overtired. It would be early to bed tonight for all the residents of Harmony House after Vilma had promised to reveal the look of the room she had been keeping hidden from view.

Eve had left a note under all the doors announcing the kitchen was now stocked, and coffee and muffins with cheese and fruit were available all evening. Full service would commence at breakfast. She did not object to being named Kitchen Supervisor but she respected the need the other women might have to cook their own meals or the occasional meal for all to share. Eve had already given thought to a system for the fridge so each person's items could be designated with a special type of storage bag. She had once worked in a busy office and knew how disruptive it could be when a worker's lunch was thrown out accidently, or eaten by a hungry person without permission.

She also expected to keep track of general supplies. It was one of the monthly expenses they would all share and, along with the costs for hydro and gas, was an unknown until several months in the house had gone by. She was determined to do whatever she could to make life easier for Hilary, who she observed to be a very conscientious woman and to whom she owed so much.

Promptly at seven o'clock, the women assembled at the door of Vilma's bedroom where she ceremonially removed the 'Keep Out' sign and threw open the door.

This interior was entirely different from any other bedroom. The first thing to command attention was the entire wall devoted to an elaborate cherry wood shelving system which allowed Vilma to display a variety of decorative objects including books and lamps. The lower level of the unit had drawers and even an attached table. The remaining walls were painted in a restful shade of green and casual furniture of a modern minimalist style was arranged near the windows, with a desk/dressing table against the wall leading to the washroom.

It took a moment or two before anyone noticed there was no bed.

"Where will you sleep, Vilma?"

She chuckled at their confusion. "This is the best part," she promised, as she walked over to the wall unit and touched a concealed spring which slowly revealed a full double bed swinging down from the unit and settling quietly on the carpet. The bed had a mattress and covers and Vilma quickly removed from the drawers two pillows, placing them on the bed. It could now be seen that the lamp on a projecting shelf had become her bedside table.

"This is amazing! You have transformed the room into a bedsitting room."

"How much more floor space you have now! It's a brilliant idea."

"Where did you find such a marvellous thing?"

Vilma gladly related the story of her search. "I wanted something different," she explained. "This is a new start in life and I wanted to have no reminders of the past. I feel I will be happy in my unusual room.

The group then moved to the kitchen dining room for more conversation and the snacks Eve had prepared. A schedule of visiting each other's rooms was discussed.

It was not long, however, before all declared the need for sleep and wandered off to their bedrooms where, surrounded by tokens of their previous lives, they slept for the first time in Harmony House.

CHAPTER 25

A month went by during which routines began to be established. A white board had to be pinned up in the kitchen so anyone needing a ride into London could see who was likely to be heading that way.

Jannice bought a first aid kit and declared she would take a course in health related issues.

Honor searched online for a bargain set of outdoor furniture and found an expensive collection, unsold from the previous summer, which the vendor was anxious to remove from his London premises in order to make space for new models. Honor negotiated a good price, inclusive of delivery and set-up and a two year warranty. Once this was accomplished, the benefits of the patio and the easy access to the basement walk-out were obvious. Honor enjoyed the company and installed a coffeemaker on a spare desk for the enjoyment of those relaxing outside.

Spring moved smoothly into summer and the grass began to grow apace. Mavis had pottered around in the raised beds planting seeds and cleaning out weeds but she was aware more had to be done. The remnants of the spring bulb display had to be dealt with before too long.

When the tall young man arrived early one morning while she was bent double picking persistent weeds from the pathways, she greeted him as a long-lost friend.

"Mrs. Ridley was kind enough to mention your front lawn needs trimming. I'm Andy Patterson. I'm a private contractor and I set out this garden some time ago. I do lawn maintenance and snow removal and I have my own equipment. If you need me at any time, here's my card."

Mavis almost kissed him. He was not only useful, but decorative, in his overalls with Green Gardens on a patch on the back, and he was quite the most handsome man she had ever seen up close. He had green eyes, slightly darker than Mavis's own, the kind of long, dark lashes that are desired by every woman born, and an even tan, indicating his outdoor lifestyle. His dark hair was short and his entire presence was workmanlike.

"When can you start?"

"Well, I do all the gardens in the crescent here. I usually come on a Wednesday, if that suits you?"

"Perfectly!"

"But we haven't discussed my rates."

"I am not in a position to quibble about that, young man. I need your help. Could you possibly manage the front lawn today, just so Mrs. Ridley won't complain?"

He knew she was joking but he also knew the lady in question and her little snide remarks.

"I think I can for that for you, Mrs ....?"

"Oh, call me Mavis. I am so pleased to meet you, Andy. Bring your contract next week and thank you a million times on behalf of all at Harmony House."

She offered her somewhat weed-stained hand and felt the strength of his grasp. He had the large hands and large booted feet of a typical tall fellow. She watched as he went back through the gap in the hedge to fetch his lawn mower. When he was gone she ran indoors, kicked off her garden shoes and nipped into the elevator in case she spread dirt inside the house.

She found her housemates in the kitchen enjoying the first coffee of the day.

"Hello and good morning," she announced. "Please bring your coffee along to the front porch. There's someone special I want you to see. He is going to be a fixture here very shortly and you need to get the full impact today."

This did not sound at all like the normally low-key Mavis. No one argued. They trooped along the passage to the front doors and out onto the covered porch where old wicker chairs had recently been found and brought home from a country auction house.

"What are we supposed to be looking at?"

"Wait one minute and you will see," Mavis replied. She had an air of suppressed excitement such as Hilary had never seen since before Peter died.

There was an indrawn breath when Andy appeared on a riding mower trailing a wagon filled with rakes and bags and garden implements. He jumped down and detached the trailer, setting it aside on the path out of the way and then, suddenly realizing he was being watched, he raised his hand in greeting and said "Hi ladies!" without a trace of embarrassment.

No one said a word while they watched him begin to carve straight lanes up and down the front lawn.

Finally, Jannice broke the silence.

"Where did you find *him*, Mavis?"

"Let's say he just popped into our lives for the foreseeable future."

"Well then, I thought our Harmony House was perfect but now I realize it needed one last special feature and today it has arrived."

"Oh, Vilma!" was the cry.

They knew she was right. A weekly dose of young and handsome Greek God was the final touch to make Harmony House absolutely perfect.

~

The story of these six women continues in **Fantasy House**.

Is true harmony possible among such different women? Now that the home of their dreams has been found, will these six different women settle into peaceful coexistence, or will their past lives continue to disturb their tranquility?

Find out more about Ruth Hay's three other series on Amazon.com, Kobo, Barnes &Noble etc. and her current writing, at www.ruthhay.com where you can sign up for a free monthly newsletter.

ALSO BY RUTH HAY

Visit www.ruthhay.com for links to all of Ruth's stories:
the Prime Time series, the Seafarers series, and the Seven
Days series!

Prime Time Series

Auld Acquaintance

Time Out of Mind

Now or Never

Sand in the Wind

With This Ring

The Seas Between Us

Return to Oban: Anna's Next Chapter

Seafarers Series

Sea Changes

Sea Tides

Gwen's Gentleman

Gwen's Choice

Seven Days Series

Seven Days There

Seven Days Back

Seven Days Beyond

Seven Days Away

Seven Days Horizons

Seven Days Destinations

Borderlines (Standalone)

Borderlines

93646827R00181

Made in the USA
Columbia, SC
15 April 2018